ESCORT

William Ed. Johnson, II

Order this book online at www.trafford.com
or email orders@trafford.com

Most Trafford titles are also available at major online book retailers.

Printed in Victoria, BC, Canada.

ISBN: 978-1-4269-2573-3 (Soft)
ISBN: 978-1-4269-2574-0 (Hard)

Library of Congress Control Number: 2010900409

Our mission is to efficiently provide the world's finest, most comprehensive book publishing service, enabling every author to experience success. To find out how to publish your book, your way, and have it available worldwide, visit us online at www.trafford.com

Trafford rev. 05/18/2010

   www.trafford.com

North America & international
toll-free: 1 888 232 4444 (USA & Canada)
phone: 250 383 6864 ♦ fax: 812 355 4082

Dedication

Melissa

I am grateful for the love you shared with me. Your insight and suggestions helped me finish this book.

Prologue

A series of dreams inspired me to write this story. All characters in this book are fictional creations of my imagination and not intended to relate to anyone living, or deceased.

Chapter 1

Crissy struggles to balance her books while trying to open the door to her classroom, when suddenly a hand reaches from behind her, she turns around, "Hey, Crissy, its Jan, remember me?"

"Yes, I remember; we had several classes together last semester, and summer school."

"It's hard to believe we are starting our senior year already." Jan replies

They sit beside each other in the back of the room.

A few moments pass, "Hello class, I'm Mr. Walker, your economics teacher; I know you are going to think this is a boring class, but I expect you to pay attention, learn, and pass my class, then you'll graduate next June."

The class drags on for thirty-five minutes, until the bell finally rings.

They leave class, Crissy reaches for Jan's arm, "What other classes are you taking Jan?"

Jan takes her out class schedule; she looks at it, "English, refresher math, PE, economics class, and several others."

Crissy looks at her class schedule, "That's great, I have some of those classes too, and we'll be taking them together. "

"Our next class is English," Jan says,

Crissy and Jan start to enter their class, when Crissy exclaims "Oh, yuck!"

"What's wrong Crissy?".

"There's Tom my former boyfriend, I don't want to sit near him because we broke up after dating a while."

"Uh oh, I hope he isn't going to cause you any problems." Jan says.

They find two desks on the opposite side of the room.

Crissy grins at Jan, "My luck plays out again; I won't be sitting by him over here."

"English class was so boring, let's have lunch now." Jan says.

They walk into the lunchroom, "Let's get sandwiches Jan."

"Did Tom even look at you Crissy?"

"No, and I don't really care."

"Were you two seriously dating?" Jan asks.

"Until I started working, then he became possessive and demanding too much of my time. I could not take his crap anymore. I told him to get lost, and broke up with him."

Crissy looks at Jan; who has a puzzled look on her face. "Tom wasn't paying my bills, buying clothes, or offering any help with future college needs. He started acting like dating was only about his needs, not mine."

"What kind of work are you doing?" Jan asks.

She picks up her sandwich, "Lets look for a private area outside to eat, and we'll talk more."

They sit together under the shade of a large tree. Crissy starts eating, she is glad there no one is nearby.

After a few moments, Jan says, "I know I could not afford those clothes you're wearing Crissy. Obviously your job must pay better than average."

"I make way better than average money Jan. I'm also saving enough to pay for my first two years of college."

"What did your parents say when you told them you were getting a job?" Jan asks.

"They asked me how many hours I would work, the wages I would make. They did not want work to affect my schoolwork. I have talked to my father privately; I did not tell him the exact nature of my work. I told him my wages would make me self sufficient, He was happy that what he paid mom for child support would be all hers."

"Do you work, just weekends only?" Jan asks.

"Yes, Saturdays, a few Sundays. I have plenty of time to study, finish home work, and of course shop!"

"I wish I had a job like yours Crissy, I certainly need new clothes, and want to save for college too."

"This work might not be right for you Jan."

"And why not?" Jan asks.

You should talk to your parents; ask them about working weekends."

"It will be hard talking to my father. He has been very distant since they divorced. He is often late paying child support, or comes up with lame excuses, and does not pay mom what he owes. He pays her a little here, and there, which pisses her off."

"We have similar problems with both of our fathers Jan, I'm sure if you told him you could start supporting yourself, he wouldn't throw a fit about you working."

"Both of them will ask me who has this job opening I could apply for Crissy."

"Old man Junkett asked me if I would find one of my girl friends to apply, of course, that includes you."

"Do any of our other classmates work for him Crissy?"

"Maybe you remember Mary; she took a summer PE class with us a couple years ago? She worked for him for quite awhile and then wanted to quit, she told me about the job. After I talked to him I watched what she did; and decided I would do it."

"I remember Mary; I didn't know her very well. Have you talked to anyone else about the job Crissy?"

"No, I haven't asked anyone yet about it. I really have not asked you Jan, I am only telling you what will be necessary to say about it to your parents, and get their permission. When they both agree, then we will talk further, and I'll explain the work in more detail to you."

"You know my parents are going to ask me to give them some details about this job Crissy. Can you at least give me a hint of what I should tell them?"

Crissy looks at Jan, "Tell them its secretary work, doing his billing, correspondence, and helping his client's with their needs, and wants."

"I suppose telling them that will work for now."

"When I get into the details about the work Jan, you must, I repeat, you must promise me to never tell anyone anything about it."

"That makes it all sounds so very secret Crissy, but I will promise you!"

"In a way Jan, in its own way, yes, we don't need everyone running to Mr. Junkett, begging him for work. He trusted Mary, he trusts me, and I must trust you!"

When school ends, the girls begin going home. Jan dreads the idea of talking to her father. She knows her mother will support her working, especially for Mr. Junkett. He is well known and respected in the business community.

Jan walks in the door, she sees her mother Judy in the living room, "Hi Jan, how was your first day of school?"

"It was ok, several boring classes. At least I met someone I knew from other classes I have taken. Do you remember me talking about Crissy?"

"You mentioned her; but you never brought her home with you."

"No, she never came home with me mom. We had classes together last year, and in summer school. Crissy told me that she has a job on weekends I wanted to talk to you and dad about it,"

Jan sits across from Judy; she studies her mother's face for a moment. "Crissy told me she fills in as a secretary for Mr. Junkett, every Saturday, and sometimes on Sunday. He pays her very well; she also assists some of his clients with their needs."

"Did Crissy explain any more to you about the kind of work he has her doing for his clients?"

"I have to presume secretary work for them too mom. He asked Crissy to look for another girl to work for him. I need both of your permission to apply for the job. If you both agree, Crissy would arrange an interview for me to talk to him. After I have an interview, I can tell you more about what I would do to help him, or his clients."

Judy leans forward, "You know very well your father will ask if you have more information about it Jan."

"I can only give either of you the limited information Crissy has told me. Dad would be glad I would make my own money, and happier that his child support would be all yours mom."

"That will give your father some relief. He hates paying us anything. He feels guilty I found out he was cheating and being responsible for our divorce Jan."

"Neither of us is responsible for his guilt, that's his problem mom."

Judy looks away, she wipes a tear from her eye, "Neither of us will ever understand why he decided to cheat, he lives with the woman he became involved with.

He dotes on her; instead, he should be more responsible to us. You know he might want her to be there with him if you two talk. If she is, she might give him her point of view and advice. That could affect his decision about you working Jan."

"I really hate this mom."

"I know you do, as much as I do Jan." Judy leans over, she rubs her hand, and they smile at one another.

"My goal is to try and make enough money for college since I probably can't rely on dad. I will suggest a park or somewhere we can meet and be alone. I don't want her tagging along, offering anything that might influence him"

"That's a good idea Jan."

"She's at work, he has the day off, it's best if I call him right now."

She goes in her room to collect her thoughts, suppress her anger, and the resentment she has for him. She dials his number; her father Jack answers, "Dad, its Jan, I hope you're doing well. I need to talk to you, could we meet alone at Parker Park?"

After a short pause, "What's on your mind Jan, what do you need to talk to me alone about? I have a very busy schedule. I'll have to arrange my time to talk to you."

Jan suppresses her anger, "Dad it's very important, I promise not to take too much of your precious time."

"I don't like that tone in your voice Jan."

"Sorry dad, it's been very stressful for me, I need your permission to apply for a job I've heard about."

After a long pause, "Alright Jan, meet me Thursday, at four, in the middle of the park by the fountain."

"I'll be there dad, and thank you, I appreciate that you're doing this for me, and please come alone."

She hangs up her phone and leaves the bedroom.

Judy is in the kitchen preparing their dinner.

She leans on the kitchen door, until Judy sees her, "You have a stressful look on your face Jan,"

"Of course mom, you know how dad can start acting up. At least he's going to meet me this Thursday at Parker Park."

"Alone?" Judy asks.

"I emphasized that I wanted him to come alone mom, he said he would. He tried to give me a guilt trip about how busy he is. He always wants to control the situation."

Judy walks over to Jan, and gives her a hug, "He has no idea what a father should be. It is difficult for him to understand what we are feeling; it is always about him. At least he said she wouldn't be with him."

"I often wonder what it was about her that attracted him in the first place mom; after all you're still very pretty."

Judy smiles at her, "I don't think about it any more Jan, I knew he was lying, something in my instinct told me that."

Jan walks into the kitchen, she sits at the table watching Judy finish cooking dinner.

Judy sits a plate in front of her. "Eat Jan, you need to keep yourself strong, I know you will be assertive enough to get his permission so you can at least apply for work. Just so you know how I feel, I fully support you."

She looks up at her; a tear runs from her eye, "Mom that means the world to me."

They eat in silence the rest of their dinner.

Judy smiles, "Your going to be alright Jan, I know that, as well as you do."

"Of course I'll be fine; I've made up my mind about that mom. I just worry about his reactions, mom. He can be difficult and so stubborn all at the same time."

Judy looks at her a moment, "We both know that Jan, just show him how mature you really are. Try to not let him see you're angry about how he has treated us."

"I will try; I'm not as angry at him since he said he's coming by himself. I really hope he does listen, instead of trying to analyze me."

She watches Judy finish putting food in the refrigerator, "Do you think dad would say I can't work mom? You seem to give me the impression he might do that."

Judy hugs her, "We both know if we make him mad, that's when he starts taking out his feelings on both of us Jan. I hope he does not do that to you. I care less what he does to me, I've learned how to ignore him, and it's better if you do the same."

Jan looks at her, "I don't want end up feeling like I have to beg him for his permission to work."

Judy gives her an anguished look, "No way, you don't have to beg him Jan Just be yourself and tell him what Crissy has told you. You can stretch the truth a little bit by telling him it might be your chance to advance if he gives you the opportunity." Judy winks her eye.

Jan smiles, "Mom, I'll plan on doing just that."

"I know you'll stand your ground Jan. Don't try going head to head with your father, he has his way of wanting to win, and will do it at all costs."

Jan gets an angry look, "I want to confront him about her, should I do it?"

Judy looks at Jan, "I would love it if you did Jan, just use your common sense. Be aware if you start asking him anything about her it could piss him off."

Jan smiles, "I know mom, but if I chose the right moment to ask him, he just might offer more information we want to know."

"We're both angry Jan, and rightfully so. Let your gut instinct tell you when it is the right moment. If you start getting angry at him then he will stop talking to you and you won't get anything from him."

"Its Mr. Junkett's policy that I have permission from both of you, since I'm only seventeen and still in school, If dad throws a big fit, and won't give me permission, then I will just wait until after my birthday."

She looks at her watch, "I'm going to bed and get some rest, good night, and I love you."

Judy gives her another hug, "I love you too Jan, sleep well. We can talk more about this, if you want to."

Jan starts walking to her room, she hugs Judy again, "You're the best mom, and your support is everything I need to succeed."

She goes into her room; thinking to herself, "Dad, I'll show you by flashing a lot of money in your face."

She mentally plays out in her mind how she should talk to her father. She knows what she should, and most important should not say. The comment Crissy made to her about helping clients and their needs mystifies her. She hopes what ever a client will need; she would be qualified to help them. She feels more secure that Crissy will be there to help her, if she needs it.

Chapter 2

Jan and Crissy meet each other Thursday, "I'm going to go talk to dad, this afternoon after class Crissy."

"Make sure you just ask for his permission to apply for a job, try to not offer him any details." Crissy says, as they walk to PE class together.

"Crissy, I know my dad, if I tell him Mr. Junkett will have a job opening soon at his business, then dad is more than likely going to give me permission, since everyone in town knows him."

Crissy stops, "Look, Jan I really hate to remind you again, but you have to watch what you say to your dad or anyone about him having a job opening up soon."

"I'm sorry, I didn't mean to offend you Crissy. I have to be honest to a degree with both of my parents. If it makes you feel better, I'll only tell them whatever you want me to about the job."

"We will talk more about it once you have his permission Jan."

They open their lockers, and take out their gym clothes.

"If you say it the right way Jan, then he'll say you can go for it, after all it'll be best for you, and your mother. Just make sure you emphasize to him that you need to make your own money."

She unbuttons her blouse and removes it, "You have a great body Jan."

Jan realizes she is looking at her, and turns red in embarrassment.

Crissy grins while she watches Jan put her sweat top on, "Your not gay are you Crissy?"

"I just wanted to tell you that you have a great looking body, and no I'm not even gay."

They spend the next hour exercising and working out together.

The bell rings, they go to the showers.

"Come on Jan, let's wash up," Crissy steps into the shower nude.

Jan hesitates; takes off her gym clothes and walks to the opposite side of the shower.

She tries to look without her noticing; when their eyes meet Crissy smiles as she washes her hair.

Jan looks down, and thinks to herself, "She is right, I do have a great looking body."

Wrapping themselves in a towel, they sit side-by-side drying their hair.

Crissy finishes and starts dressing.

Jan watches Crissy pull her panties on. She has a totally shaved pubic area.

Crissy finishes putting on her bra; pulls her jeans up, and puts her top on. "Jan, don't worry about what I said about your body, you're beautiful, so am I and our bodies will make both of us major money."

Crissy takes her by the hand, "You are the friend I told about this job Jan. There will be things you're going to have to pay attention to, in order to make more money, but we will discus that in more detail later."

"I'll let you know what happens after I talk to dad Crissy. Now I have to get going to Parker Park, if I'm on time that will please him."

"Call me early Saturday morning. Let me know you get his permission, I will tell Mr. Junkett when I go into work. Get going so you are not late and good luck!"

She gives Crissy a big hug.

She runs out and catches the bus that goes by Parker Park.

She nervously looks at her watch, and thinks to herself, "It's only three thirty and even with all the stops I should be at the park by three fifty five."

She sits behind the driver looking at familiar places in town while the bus heads to the park.

The bus driver tells her, "Next stop is Parker Park Miss."

"Thanks," She looks at her watch, thinking to herself "Thank goodness the bus was fast today, I won't have to rush quite so much."

She gets off at her stop, and starts walking to the fountain, she hopes her father is waiting for her.

Almost midway into the park, she hears his voice, "Jan, over here."

She sees him walking towards her from the rear exit of the park.

He walks up and gives her a hug then looks at his watch. "You're early, Jan."

"Of course dad it's important we met today and talk about my job."

"Let's sit over there," he says, pointing to a bench by the fountain.

"At least we will have privacy dad."

Jan watches him looking around the park.

"Are you looking for someone dad?"

"No Jan, I'm just nervous about meeting you today."

She takes his hand; and looks at him, "Dad I need your permission to apply for a job."

"Alright, tell me who has a job, and where you would work."

"Crissy told me that Mr. Junkett is opening a position for another girl at his business. He asked her if she knew anyone that was looking for work. She thought I would be interested, and mentioned it to me. She said it's his policy that I have both of your permission to apply because I'm a minor and still in school."

11

"You met Crissy at school?"

"Yes, we have had classes together before in other semesters, and this year too."

Still looking tense, he leans back, and looks at her. "Did Crissy say what the work schedule would be Jan?"

"Late afternoon, early evenings every Saturday dad, I would be home by nine at the very latest. Once in a while she said we might work on Sunday."

"Did she say if he would have you doing the same work she is?"

"Crissy said we will do his billing, correspondence, and help his clients with their needs dad. You should see her; she has very nice and expensive clothes, and is saving for college too."

Jack smiles and she relaxes more. "You're sure you would have time to study?"

"Yes, just working weekends, I will dad, I promise. I really need the job, and the experience."

"Did your mother say it's alright with her that you could apply for the job Jan?"

"I have her full support in any effort to better myself. Besides dad, working will take a lot of pressure off her. She will be able to use everything you pay in child support for her."

He smiles some more while looking at her. He takes her hand in his, "You're growing up so fast Jan; I'm impressed with your mature attitude. I don't have a problem with you working as long as it doesn't affect your school work."

Jan breaks into a large grin; she gives him a hug, and kisses his cheek.

She sits back watching his eyes glancing at the park exit, "Mom and me wonder why you decided to cheat, and leave us for that woman."

He looks at her, "It didn't just happen on a lark Jan."

He looks at his watch, "I really don't have to justify my decision to you, or your mother Jan. We fell out of love almost as quick as we fell into love."

Jan suppresses her anger looks away, and then looks back at him. "Your right dad, nothing you say will alleviate our hurt, nor our anger. We all have to rebuild our lives."

He defensively crosses his arms across his chest and sits back on the bench.

She knows by the look on his face, that he is becoming more anxious. She stares at him, stopping herself from exploding her anger at him. She knows this is not the place, or the time to do so.

They sit for a moment staring at one another. "Jan, I still love you, and in a different way I will always love your mother, I couldn't love your mother the way she needed me to. We out grew one another, it was best for both of us that we moved on in life separately."

"With another woman and cheat on mom dad, that is how you moved on as you say?"

"I know, I know Jan, there isn't any excuse that you, or your mother would understand."

She looks at her watch, "I better go home dad; mom will be worried if I'm late for dinner."

Jan leans towards Jack, she forces herself to give him another hug, "Thanks again for meeting with me dad. I appreciate that you took the time to talk to me."

"Good luck Jan, let me know if you get an interview, and get hired."

He gets up from the bench at the same time she does. He smiles, and walks back to the rear entrance of the park. Jan wipes tears from her face, she stops walking to the park entrance.

Looking back, she sees him, and the woman he left her mother for hugging in the distance.

"Damn him," Jan thinks to herself. "He couldn't even honor my request to meet me alone. He had her waiting for him here while we were talking. No wonder he was getting so anxious."

The bus pulls up; she gets on, silently sitting and staring as it pulls away from the park.

Jan gets off the bus and walks home.

She opens the door and walks in; her mother is busy cooking dinner in the kitchen.

Judy can tell by looking at her she is angry and stressed.

Neither of them says anything for a few moments, "Sit down Jan; I'll have dinner ready in a few moments."

"Dad met me, but would you believe he had her waiting for him by the exit of the park?"

"I hate to say yes, but I do believe that would be something your father would do Jan.

Did you see her when you started to walk into the park?"

"No, it was while I was leaving, I saw them embrace and walk off together. She probably waited where she knew I would not look for dad, and see her."

"I hope that she does not try to influence your father Jan. I'm sure he's getting an ear full from her now that he has told her about his decision."

Judy sits next to her at the table.

Jan takes a few bites of food, "Very good dinner mom, I hope you won't be mad. I am not that hungry tonight after dad did not honor my request to come alone. That is upsetting me so much it pretty much killed my appetite."

Judy runs her fingers through Jan's hair, "Eat what you can Jan. I'm so sorry your father did that to you."

"Us mom, us, he did it to us. I managed to tell him how hurt we are. He dodged my question, about why he decided to cheat and leave with her. All he had to say was that he did not have to justify anything to either of us. He became more defensive, as I got angrier. I managed to control myself, that wasn't the reason I went to see him."

"Did he give you his permission to apply for work at Mr. Junkett's?"

"Yes, he said I could. I thought after I told him how we felt he would change his mind and say no, but he did not."

Judy smiles at her. "Your father never ceases to amaze me. When are you going to tell Crissy?"

"I told her I would call her Saturday morning. I am hoping she can meet me before she goes to work. I want her to mention me to Mr. Junkett."

"I am sure she will be glad to know you have both of our permission Jan.

She sits playing with her food.

"Do you want any more dinner, or are you finished Jan?"

"I'm finished mom, I ate a little, and that will be enough for now. I'm going to my room now and rest."

Judy sees how drained her face looks, "Yes Jan, get some rest, it has been a stressful day for you."

Jan wraps her plate in tin foil; she places it in the refrigerator. "I might be a little hungrier later, so I'll save this mom."

"Good night Jan, rest well."

"I will mom; I'll talk to you in the morning."

Walking slowly to her room she opens the door and looks around it. She undresses, puts on her nightgown, and lies on her bed. Her tears keep falling as she hopes sleep will overtake her racing mind and thoughts. She keeps thinking how her father disrespected her by bringing that woman with him. She keeps looking at her clock wishing the hours would pass faster.

Saturday morning Jan wakes to see it is only eight am. "I'll have time to shower and clean up before I call Crissy."

She gets out of the shower, and sits in front of her bureau mirror blow-drying her hair.

She nervously looks at the clock it is finally nine.

She calls Crissy, her mother answers the phone, "Hello Laura, its Jan, is Crissy home?"

"Hi Jan, I'll go get her, hold on please."

Crissy picks up the phone, "Hi Jan, do you have news for me?"

"Yes, I do, dad will let me apply for the job. Can we meet this afternoon before you go to work? I would like to know some more about the job. If I like what you tell me, will you tell Mr. Junkett about me this afternoon and ask him when I can get an interview?"

"Lets meets for lunch today at Snider's hot dog stand at eleven, we will talk while we eat. I will tell you more about the work then. If you decide you want to do the job, I'll tell him and let you know when he wants to interview you."

"Ok Crissy, I'll see you at eleven, that's a good time for me."

Jan gets dressed she walks into the kitchen.

Judy sees Jan, "Did you talk to Crissy this morning Jan?"

"Yes, and she'll meet me at eleven today and we will talk during lunch."

"Jan, I know how excited you will be if you are interviewed for the job, but don't get your hopes up too much until Crissy explains more about it to you. Then you can decide if you are even interested. Keep in mind that Mr. Junkett might have you doing different work than she is."

"I am hoping mom, but I also have an open mind that I might not have some skill his work requires."

Judy looks at Jan, "You took classes in school that taught you a lot, and you're good at typing."

"I'm glad now I took classes learning how to operate copy machines, fax machines and other important business machines."

Judy gets up; she looks at Jan, and asks, "Crissy didn't say if he might have you work with something you're not familiar with?"

"Not really mom, she was vague, if I get the interview with Mr. Junkett, I'm sure he would tell me exactly what he wants me to do. Of course, she has been there for a while, and could teach me about anything my classes didn't cover."

"You're lucky she has been there for a while and would be willing to help you out Jan."

Jan finishes her breakfast; she looks at the clock in the living room, "Its ten thirty mom, so I had better get to the bus stop and go."

Chapter 3

Jan gets off the bus; she walks the short distance to Snider's hot dog stand. Crissy is sitting at one of the tables. "Hi Crissy, thanks for coming and talking to me today, I really appreciate it."

"Want a hot dog, my treat?" Crissy asks.

"I'm not really that hungry, but I'll have lemonade if you're buying."

Crissy buys herself a hot dog, a drink. She gives Jan her lemonade; they sit together. Crissy starts eating her hot dog Jan sips on her lemonade.

Crissy wipes her mouth with a napkin. "I told you Jan; this work might not be your thing, or what you want to do. I'll explain it to you some more, but again I really need your promise that you will not tell anyone."

"Sure, Crissy, I told you before that you have my promise to keep secret about it, I know it's important to you."

Crissy finishes her hot dog she sips her drink. "Remember when I said you have a beautiful body?"

"I don't understand, why is my body being beautiful that important if I work for Mr. Junkett?"

Crissy pauses, she drinks again, she looks directly at Jan. "I only gave you a small hint about what I do Jan. Your body will be your moneymaker, mine certainly is. I mentioned that work involves us taking care of his clients needs Jan. His clients are wealthy businesspersons. When they come into town, they want entertainment. We give it to them and they pay us very well for it."

"Entertainment, just what kind of entertainment do they want?"

Crissy glances around, and Jan feels her getting more nervous. "I told you secretary work, that's what you will always tell your parents your doing. But the reality is we entertain them nude, and more Jan."

Jan feels her face getting red; she looks at Crissy, "So you're telling me we will be going naked in front of a bunch of strangers Crissy?"

"Not a bunch, right now it is only one man, but he wants to bring a friend along in the near future, that's why he asked me to find another girl, so his other client would have entertainment too."

"Before I began working, Mary told me what I'm telling you, she said I could come with her and watch, and not be harassed. I went with her, I felt comfortable, and starting working after she left."

Jan sits in silence, feeling herself getting numb, "Both of us dance, strip, and exactly what did you mean when you said "and more?" What will his clients want us to do for them?"

"A strip tease gets them going Jan. Eventually we will go to separate private rooms with them. Your man will offer you money to have sex with him. The amount he pays you depends on what you agree to do. When you accept his money he expects you to follow through on the agreement."

Jan glances around Crissy takes her hand. "No one, me, Mr. Junkett, or his clients are going to try and force you into doing anything Jan."

"I don't know if I could do it Crissy, I admit the idea of going and watching you sounds exciting."

"The idea of seeing me nude with a man turns you on, doesn't it Jan?" Jan turns red she looks away from her.

A few moments pass, "Are we called another name for doing this besides strippers, sex slaves, or whores?"

"Crissy leans towards Jan; and looks at her, "Escort, we are called escorts.""

Jan looks at Crissy; she knows her face is bright red from embarrassment. "I've heard that name before, isn't an escort considered a prostitute, but called that name so she doesn't have stigma for selling her body?"

"Jan, what we do is provide sensual companionship to the man we are with. Escorts do not watch the time they spend with them. We help him feel comfortable, give him a strip show, massage, talk, and listen to him. We make sure he feels better by satisfying all of his needs, including sexual. Prostitutes will set a time limit for their client, like an hour, they rush to get him off and gone. I am making five hundred dollars a weekend doing what Nick asks me to do."

"That is a lot of money for a few hours of work. Does Nick ever ask you to get kinky, or do things that are turn offs to you Crissy?"

"Right from the beginning when I met him, I made it clear that we would both talk openly, and both agree on the type of sex he wanted. If I did not agree, he did not try to convince me otherwise.

I'm sure he has told his friend of this arrangement. Its money for sex Jan, that is what we do.

I told you this work might not be right for you. The men want sex; they will tell you their wife supposedly does not have it with them anymore.

Mr. Junkett provides it, and the men pay us damn well for having it with them."

Jan looks at Crissy, "Do the men ever want unprotected sex, without a condom?"

Crissy laughs, "They will offer you more money for that, so you should be on birth control, which will be your responsibility."

"What if I don't want to have sex without them wearing a condom Crissy?"

"You simply tell him, no, that isn't something I do, you must wear a condom.

Mr. Junkett has spoken to Nick, so if his friend gets too insistent and disrespects either of us, he would be told to leave immediately."

"Does Mr. Junkett watch you when you have sex with Nick?"

"We go into a private room that has a speaker in it, in case I needed to call him. If I did call, only then would he open the door, and come in to confront him, otherwise he doesn't watch or listen to us."

Jan feels her head swimming with confusion and shock at the same time. "I really need the money, but to get it that way, it is against my morals Crissy."

"Was mine too Jan, until I went with Mary and I saw her come home that night with five hundred bucks."

"Why did she quit if she was making as much as you're making Crissy?"

"She wasn't really specific, I didn't press her for a lot of details of why she wanted to quit."

"How many men did Mary meet with when she was working? Did she tell you anything about them, like if they were rough with her?"

"The first guy she met there started getting rough, beating and trying to force her into having kinky sex with him. She told Mr. Junkett, and he made him leave."

"Do you ever find yourself having enough of this work Crissy?"

"There are times I go there and don't feel sexy or want sex, but when Nick starts taking all that money out of his wallet, I put myself into a state of mind where my body is there, my mind is elsewhere."

"I need to think about this Crissy, my head's really hurting. I would have to be more than sure I could do this before I can obligate myself."

"Remember Jan, I told you that you can come, observe and watch. If you didn't want to go any further, that's up to you."

"Do you think that Nick's friend would be there?"

"Nick said he wants to come sometime soon, so I will tell Mr. Junkett I have talked to you. You can go with me and watch us before his friend starts coming with him, then you will have time to think about it."

"If I went with you to watch, and his friend was there and offered me money, all I have to do is tell him no, and that's it, nothing would happen?"

"Right, Jan, you have Mr. Junkett's and my assurance nothing would happen."

Jan looks at her watch, "I better let you go, we have talked more than an hour and I don't want you to be late."

"I did need to ask one other thing Jan, you're eighteen now?"

"I will be on December fifteenth, so it's not hard to forget," Jan replies with a laugh.

"Damn, Mr. Junkett insists that we're both eighteen. You are going to have to wait; he will need to verify your age. No minors protect him and his clients."

They walk to the bus stop, "I'll go ahead and tell him you might be interested. Maybe the other client won't come with Nick until after your birthday."

"I'll tell mom that my periods have been irregular, she can call Doctor Burke, and he will prescribe birth control pills. I'm thinking positive about our talk today, starting birth control will help me be ready in case Nick's friend comes after my birthday."

Jan hugs Crissy, and boards the bus home. She sits alone, thinking about her conversation with Crissy. The bus stops near her home, Jan opens her door. Judy is watching her favorite soap opera.

Jan sits next to her, "Was Crissy happy you can apply for the job now, Jan?"

"Of course, only complication is, Mr. Junkett requires me to be eighteen when I do apply. I'll have to wait until after my birthday."

"At least it isn't far off; and you will have more time to refresh any skills you might need for the job,"

Jan pauses, she feels her body tense, "I need another favor mom; I'm having irregular periods, which concern me, can I go see Doctor Burke for an exam?"

"Your taking after me Jan, I had the same thing."

"When I start working, I'll take care of the extra expense mom, so please don't let that concern you,"

Judy walks to the kitchen. "We have plenty of leftovers for dinner tonight or do you want me to make you something else Jan?"

"Leftovers are fine mom, my appetite has returned."

She sits and watches Judy cooking, "You look like your lost in thought Jan, everything alright?"

Jan looks up at her, "A lot to absorb about the job mom, I told Crissy that I would tell her for sure after my birthday."

"Did Crissy tell you something about the job that's making you have second thoughts about it?" Judy asks her in a concerned voice.

Jan shifts nervously in her chair, "Not really, Crissy explained a little bit about the job, what Mr. Junkett would require, and what his clients would expect from both of us."

Judy stands at the stove stirring in the pans, "Is something about what his clients require bothering you Jan? You seem very nervous and appear a little upset about all of this."

"Most of being upset comes from my period problem. I also got frustrated that I can't go for an interview until I'm eighteen."

Judy comes over and gives her a hug. "Hormone time is a bitch Jan, we both know that. I'll call Doctor Burke in the morning, to make you an appointment as soon as possible so they stop affecting you so much."

Judy sit is a plate in front of Jan she begins to eat. "Dinner is really good tonight, perfect choice of leftovers mom," Judy and Jan eat in silence the rest of their meal.

They finish eating when the phone rings.

Judy answers the phone. "Jan, it's your father, he wants to ask you a couple more questions."

"I'll take his call in my room mom."

She picks up her phone hearing her mother hang up. "Hello dad, what's on your mind?"

"I was curious if you told Crissy you can work, and when you're getting an interview?"

"Mr. Junkett requires me to be eighteen before I can apply, or work for him dad."

"That's understandable Jan."

"Mom said you had some more questions for me dad, what were they?"

"I was wondering if Crissy told you any more about what you would do for his clients."

"Crissy said that if one or two of his clients happened to be there, that we were to help them with their paperwork, or other needs they might have dad."

Jack is silent for a moment, "That sounds like old man Junkett, he has you two girls playing a low wage secretary He is rumored to be pretty cheap when it comes to paying his help."

"I don't know what he pays his secretary dad. Crissy did tell me he pays her better than average wages. I hope to have a chance to work for him after my birthday, making as much as she does."

"He is probably willing to pay you two more because your teens, and pretty, your both eye candy for the old scrooge."

Jan stops herself from telling him about Crissy making five hundred dollars a weekend.

"Did Crissy talk to you about anything else that you would need for the job Jan?"

"Not really dad, just normal skills, typing working with fax machines, copy machines or other things an office uses, thankfully both of us took classes for all them."

"If the job is still available after your birthday, make sure you have a resume to give him when you interview."

"I'm planned on preparing a resume with all my skills listed on it. If something comes up I need to be concerned about, Crissy will let me know prior to an interview."

"I'm happy for you Jan, I really am, I hope and wish the best for you."

"Thanks dad, I'll be fine, and I appreciate your concerns. I hope I answered your questions dad, and helped you understand what I know about the job at this point."

"I have no other questions. I appreciate your telling me what you know; I feel I understand more now Jan, good night."

"Good night dad."

She wants to confront her father about bringing and embracing his woman when they talked. She pauses and holds on to that thought as she hangs up her phone.

She walks out of her room; Judy is watching television in the living room.

She hears Jan approaching "Everything alright with you and your father Jan?"

"Yes mom, he told me to prepare a resume, which I told him I was going to do. I told him a little more about how I might help Mr. Junkett's clients."

"You look a lot less stressed at least Jan."

"Dad understands mom, that when I know more then I will tell you both what I find out. I'm going to get busy on my resume mom, so I'll say good night, and thanks for being my mother, and my best friend."

Judy smiles and reaches out with her arms; Jan gives her a big hug and kiss.

"Good night Jan, I'll let you know when Doctor Burke can see you after I call his office in the morning."

Jan turns while walking to her room and smiles at her. She opens her door and goes into her room thinking to herself, "I really need that work, but I understand his client could come early, and Crissy will have to ask another girl."

She knows a resume is not necessary if she works with her. She realizes she might watch her, not want to be an escort. She starts looking at records of classes that will look good on her resume; she will not have to explain anything more to her parents, if she has it ready.

Chapter 4

She stands outside the kitchen listening to Judy on the phone talking to the Doctor's nurse. She walks into the kitchen as she hangs up.

"Jan, Doctor Burke can see you this Wednesday at ten am, will that make you miss any classes?"

"I have late afternoon classes, so I won't miss any mom."

Judy stirs in a pot; she turns to look at Jan who has seated herself at the table. "I told the nurse you were having trouble with your periods being regular, she said she would tell Doctor Burke."

"Alright mom, Doctor Burke will check me out thoroughly, since we just began school. What's that you're cooking mom?"

"Oatmeal, would you like some?"

"Just give me a small bowl full mom; I'm cutting back a little bit."

"Don't be starting one of those crazy fad diets Jan, starving your self can lead to trouble."

She stirs the oatmeal with her spoon, "I'm not starving myself mom, just cutting back a little. I've got to get going I don't want to be late for class." She says looking at her watch.

Judy smiles, walks over and gives her a hug, "Have a good day at school Jan, I'll see you later today. Did you have a special request on what you want me to make for dinner?"

She looks at Judy as she is heading for the door, "Not really mom, everything you cook is great, so you make the choice and I'll eat, I promise to not cut back too much."

Judy smiles at her as she leaves the house.

She catches the bus and sits silently in her seat. Before she realizes it, the bus pulls up to her stop, Crissy is waiting for her

She steps off the bus, "Good morning Crissy, I hope you're doing alright today?"

Crissy walks up and gives her a hug. "Good to see you, did you have a nice weekend Jan?"

They start to walk to class, "Not a bad weekend, and good news, I'm going to the Doctor Wednesday morning. I will be able to pick up my prescription that day."

Crissy pulls on her arm and they stop walking.

Crissy looks at her and asks, "Made up your mind so fast about the job already Jan?"

Jan starts to walk, Crissy beside her, "I'm still thinking about it, and if it is still available after my birthday

I want to be ready."

Crissy suddenly stops and stares, and grabs onto her sleeve. Jan sees Tom is waiting outside their classroom door.

Crissy puts her head down avoiding eye contact with him and they start to walk into class.

"Hello Crissy," he says, putting his arm across the doorway.

Crissy looks up at him, "You're blocking our way Tom, please put your arm down and leave us alone."

He drops his arm, Crissy and Jan walk by him into class, "Look I'm sorry Crissy, can I talk to you after class?"

Crissy and Jan stop, they look at him, Crissy says, "Tom, I don't want to be alone with you if we do talk."

He gets an angry disgusted look on his face he looks at them walking to their seats, "I'll wait outside after class for both of you, and let me know then if you will talk to me."

They sit at their desks; Jan reaches for her hand, giving it a squeeze, Crissy smiles. Mr. Walker enters class and goes to his desk, picks up his attendance list. He looks at everyone marking names of who is present, or absent.

The bell rings; everyone gets up and starts to walk out of class. Tom waits a few feet away from the door for them to leave. Jan holds on to her while they leave class, neither of them look at him.

He starts walking beside them. They begin walking faster trying to ignore him.

In a loud voice he says "Crissy, can I at least have one moment of your time?"

Crissy and Jan pause, they both look at him, "I told you that you have to talk to Jan and me together.

Why is it so important that you suddenly need to talk to me now? I thought I made it very clear, I didn't want to be your girlfriend anymore?"

He looks at them, after a few moments of silence, he says, "Look Crissy, I want to at least apologize to you, and ask if there is anyway we can start over?"

Crissy feels herself tense, she grabs harder onto Jan's arm.

While walking, she says, "Tom, what we had, is over; I want you to understand that. I am working I make my own money. I couldn't give you the time you wanted."

He looks at her, "I really care about you Crissy, and I want to show you how much."

Crissy takes in a deep breath, she manages to look at his face, "You got very demanding and wanted to control me, manage my time, that was selfish, and you weren't offering to help me Tom."

"We were going together; I was your boyfriend, isn't it reasonable that we needed more than several dates to learn more about each other?"

Crissy gives Tom a sarcastic look, "We went out, we had a couple dates, I told you I was going to be working weekends. Suddenly you and your needs became important, instead of mine Tom."

She and Jan continue walking together to the bus stop.

"You didn't offer me any alternatives that were workable. All you did was whine about not spending more of my time with you Tom."

He stops walking; and looks at them, "I realize now how important college is to you. I have grown up Crissy, and I hoped you would see how much. I am very sorry for how I acted then."

She looks at him, "I still want you to leave me alone Tom, go on with your life, I am mine. I'm sure there is a girl out there who will take your crap, I don't have to."

"Hell of an attitude Crissy, I'm not giving you crap, can't you understand that I wanted you to have my apology and see a difference in me?"

Crissy feels herself tense with anger. She keeps walking with Jan, they do not look at him, "It's over Tom, finished, and I accept your apology. I do not have the time or energy to give you what you need from me. If we did get back together, eventually you would start wanting me to spend more time with you. You would get mad I was not paying enough attention to you. Eventually you would go right back to your old ways."

"I get your point Crissy; I'll leave you alone. I have made an effort to change. Your assumption that I would go back to my old ways is wrong. I'll regretfully respect your decision, and I wish you well in life, good bye."

He walks away; and does not look back at them walking the opposite direction.

Jan notices her wiping tears from her eyes. "You still care about him, don't you Crissy?"

She quickly wipes her face with a tissue and looks at her, "Yes, I always will care about him Jan; he was my very first love. I couldn't afford to let him stand in the way of my efforts."

"I don't know him as well as you do Crissy, but I felt, he was being sincere, when he said he has changed, at least he also apologized to you."

"He was sincere, I couldn't let him find out what I'm doing to make money, and he would never understand my being an escort Jan."

The bus pulls up; she hugs Crissy and gets on. She sits and watches her slowly walking away. Jan feels in her heart that she is sorry that she asked him to get lost.

She opens her economics book, reading the lesson Mr. Walker gave her to finish. She keeps thinking about her appointment with the Doctor.

The bus pulls up to the stop she gets off and starts walking home. When she opens the door, Judy is busy working on papers in the living room. "Hi mom, it looks like you have homework too?"

She looks up, "I'm getting paid to finish up some work at home. I'll be starting dinner soon; we will be having navy beans with pork, is that alright?"

She laughs, "Do you want me to have gas mom?"

Judy puts down her papers, she looks at her, "Was it a good day at school Jan?"

"Not bad, Crissy had a confrontation with her former boyfriend Tom. I backed her up so he wouldn't try to pull any of his nonsense."

Judy gets a puzzled look on her face, "You've never mentioned him, what was their problem Jan?"

She helps her put dishes and silverware on the table, "He wanted too much control over her life after she started working."

"Some men just don't want to be understanding. Your father started wanting me to be something I could not be. He thinks he has found that with the woman he cheated and left with."

Jan pauses at the table looking at Judy. "Not all men are bad there are good men out there.

We all hope to find a good man and keep him. It's supposed to be a team effort, isn't it?"

Judy is stirring the food on the stove "Yes, it's a team effort, in the beginning it's all about sex. He wants it constantly; the woman complies with his desires. Then the reality of life sets in, they both need to work, pay bills and eventually take care of babies they create."

"Crissy didn't say anything to me about Tom demanding sex. They had several dates, but when she started working, he became more and more resentful she wasn't devoting more time to him."

Judy gets a disgusted look on her face, "That all most sounds exactly how your father acted. After you were born; he became resentful that I needed to take care of you."

"I hope that when a man comes into my life that he will respect me, understand me and be compassionate to my needs as much as I would his."

Judy sits two plates on the table, "Lets eat dinner Jan, I hope you like it."

She takes a couple bites watching Judy. After swallowing she says, "I like what you made for dinner mom, everything you cook is great."

"I'm glad you enjoy it Jan. You have a great man in your imagination; I hope he comes true in real life. When I met and fell in love with your father, we were so much in love that it was almost pathetic. At some point in our lives, we seemed to out grow one another Jan."

"That's what dad said to me when we were at the park. Too bad, both of you did not recognize what was going on in time to stop and rediscover the reasons why you wanted to be together. There will always be good and bad times in life, and a marriage. If both dedicate themselves and fight together, it makes them stronger, am I wrong to think that mom?"

"You're wise beyond your years Jan, very wise, if any good comes out of our divorce, its lessons about life and its realities you have learned to apply to your future." Judy says with a smile.

"I don't want my reality disintegrating into what you and dad are living right now mom."

Jan pauses; she wipes a tear from her eye. "I have an image in my mind of marriage, being a good wife, have a great husband and children; those are things in my future. I need to work, get an education, and then I hope it will come true when the time is right."

"You have a great dream Jan, an even greater image in your mind just as I did when I was your age. The sad fact is those things occurred they happened. Your father and I lived that life, and then it fell apart."

Jan finishes her dinner; she takes her plate to the sink. She sees Judy wiping tears from her eyes.

"I'm sorry mom I didn't mean to upset you."

"You didn't upset me Jan, I was crying about the happy memories your father and I had."

"Mom, we have both wished for things to be different. I remember stories that you read to me when I was little. One story was a fairy tale about a knight in silver armor on his white horse swooping up his love and riding into the sunset forever. It was only a fairy tale, and fairy tales end the way we hope our own life will end."

Judy gives her a hug then picks up her plate putting it into the sink, "I love you, and in his own way your father loves you Jan. Nothing that has happened between your father and I was your fault. Both of us woke up and felt we were living with a stranger."

"I'm glad you said that mom, when you and dad started talking about divorcing, I did blame myself, I thought I could have been the reason your marriage was failing. I thought I should have done more, or said more and that would have stopped the divorce from happening."

"Oh dear Jan, nothing could be more wrong than you feeling that way. I am glad you told me, I hope I have made it clear that we never blamed you."

Jan kisses her on the cheek. Judy finishes washing the dishes, putting them away, "You have a mature outlook so early in life Jan, you were forced to grow up fast after everything happened between myself and your father. At least you're mature enough now to look back and see both of our mistakes and learned from them."

"I don't see what mistakes you made mom, you have made every effort. Dad has failed to learn how his mistakes would affect us."

"I hope Crissy will find a good man for her needs, just as you are hoping for the same Jan.

What both of your fathers have done almost makes them twins."

"Crissy never has told me if her father cheated, so I don't know for sure if that's why her parents divorced."

"It really makes no difference Jan, relationships can start coming apart at the seams. When ours began to tear apart, I tried everything to repair it and put back together.

I made every effort to let him know I loved him and would always be there for him. I blamed myself a short time after our divorce for his cheating. I felt that somehow I failed him, by not doing more Jan."

She looks at Judy, "You did all you could mom, and it was dad who failed not just you, but us."

Judy wipes tears from her eyes, "You were so young Jan; I knew it wasn't fair to you. I should have told you then that nothing happening between us was your fault. I regret not doing that more than our marriage failing."

They hug, "We can't change the past mom. I know now it wasn't my fault, that helps me to start feeling better in a lot of ways."

"Jan I really love the woman you're growing up to be, you don't hold grudges or animosity in your heart."

"You have done your best mom; I can't find all the words to say how much I appreciate you. Now if I get a good job I can take care of myself, so all the money dad pays, you can use for yourself."

"Jan, no matter what you and I will be alright, despite your father or anyone else!"

"No matter what mom, I am determined to finish my senior year, make good money, and go to college. I want to finish college before even thinking about marriage, children and all the responsibilities."

"At least you have a plan Jan, stick to it, love happens, it can come when you least expect it."

"I'm off to bed now mom, I'm glad we had this talk, and further understanding."

Judy walks up to her hugging and kissing her cheek, "Sleep well Jan, I'll talk to you in the morning."

Chapter 5

Jan walks into the kitchen; Judy is stirring oatmeal in a pan. "I've fixed you pancakes Jan, did you want oatmeal instead?"

Jan sighs and sits at the table looking at her. "That will be sufficient mom, thank you."

They finish eating in silence.

She takes her plate to the sink to wash it. Judy is right behind her, "Care to wash my bowl too Jan?"

She turns, takes her bowl and washes it. "Jan, you should get to the bus stop so you will be on time to see Doctor Burke."

She looks at her watch, "I won't be late mom, and I'll call Crissy real quick and remind her that I am going to the Doctor this morning."

"Did you tell her why you're going to see the Doctor Jan?" Judy asks with a quizzed look on her face.

"None of her business mom, I'm not one to discuss my period problems with other girls at school."

Judy smiles at her, "I didn't discuss those things with girls I knew either."

She picks up her purse; she looks in it making sure she has enough change for bus fare to the Doctor's office and back home.

"If the Doctor gives you a prescription Jan, just call me, I'll call the pharmacy and use my credit card to pay for it. You can start taking them as soon as possible, to get relief from your cramping."

"I'll pay you back when I start work mom, please don't worry that they will be an extra expense."

"I wasn't worried Jan, we'll be fine."

Jan goes to her room and looks at her watch; she needs to leave by five minutes after nine.

She dials Crissy's number. "Hi Crissy, I'll be going to the Doctors soon, so I cannot talk long."

"I was just about to call you; I'm afraid I have some bad news for you. Mary just called me letting me know that she asked Mr. Junkett if he would let her come back to work. He told her Nick just called asking if he hired an extra girl, if so, he would bring his friend with him this weekend. It was her luck that she just happened to call him after they finished talking."

"Damn!" Jan feels herself tense. "You didn't tell her he wanted you to look for another girl did you Crissy?"

"Today was the first time in almost a month that we have talked to one another. When she quit I thought that she was finished working there for good."

Jan feels herself wanting to cry, she restrains herself, "Well, she might not stick it out. She left once before, more than likely its possible she is will do it again. I hope she decides to leave after my birthday, and then I'll have a chance."

"If you want to change your mind Jan, it is fine with me."

"No, I'm still going to my appointment Crissy. Nick or the other man might bring another friend and I could be with him."

"I'll ask him if they know anyone else that would be interested in coming. You still should consider watching Nick and I first Jan."

"If they do Crissy, tell them I'll be available after mid December because until then I am committed to a school project. Maybe after my birthday I will watch, anyhow I must go now, I don't want to be late getting to the Doctor, please keep me informed."

"Bye Jan, sorry to have given you bad news, I at least wanted to be fair to you."

She runs to her bus stop, getting to it just as it arrives. Sitting by a window, she watches her world go by. Wiping tears from her eyes, she wonders if she is going through all of this for nothing. She tries not being upset at Mary's decision, she has her reasons, and neither her or Crissy can predict exactly what she might do now.

Jan thinks to herself, "Maybe she will quit after my birthday that would be perfect timing for me. I'm glad I don't have to wait that long, two months isn't that far off."

The bus pulls up by the Doctor's office she is on time. Jan goes to the reception desk; signs her name on the register.

The nurse walks in and sees her, "Hello Jan, your mother called, and gave us your insurance information, and verbal permission for the Doctor to examine you."

Jan glances around the Doctor's office she is happy that no one is familiar.

She would not want to have anyone wondering why she was there. She picks up a magazine to read while waiting.

The nurse calls her; she puts the magazine down, and follows her to an examination room. The nurse takes her temperature, blood pressure, and checks her weight; she is pleased to have lost four pounds.

The nurse looks at her, "Your mother said you were having period problems?"

"I've been having irregular periods, a lot of cramping, and irregular bowel movements. It's something I inherited from mom; I hope the Doctor can give me help for those problems."

"No other concerns I should tell the Doctor about?"

"No, nothing else that's all I needed to see him for."

The nurse finishes writing in her chart, "Doctor Burke will be with you in a few moments Jan, please put this examination gown on, and remove your panties and any tampon or sanitary napkin."

She watches as the nurse leaves.

The door opens and the Doctor walks in with his nurse behind him. "Jan, good to see you today, my nurse told me you're having irregular periods and harder than usual cramping?"

She smiles, "It's good to see you too Doctor. What your nurse told you is correct."

He finishes writing in her chart, "Get up on that table and I'm going to gently push your abdominal and pubic areas. If you have pain, or discomfort in them, please let me know."

She struggles to get comfortable; the coldness of the table on her butt sends chills through her body.

He washes his hands, puts on gloves, and walks over to the table. "Jan, I know it's not comfortable, but I need you to lie back on the table."

She lies down holding on to her gown. The nurse puts a pillow under her head. He puts a blanket over her, and starts pressing with his fingers. "Jan, what part of your period do you start having irregular bowel movements?"

"Usually when it begins, then after several days, I'm back to being regular."

He keeps pressing lower, Jan tenses in anticipation. She looks at the nurse who smiles at her.

Suddenly she says, "Oh, where you're pushing now, is very sensitive Doctor, right there," she lifts her head up off the pillow trying to see where his hand is.

He looks at her and says, "My hand is right above your ovaries, around there can be more sensitive during your period Jan."

"Since these problems became more frequent Doctor it has been a lot more sensitive there."

He continues pressing her abdomen while his nurse watches her for reactions. Jan flinches again when he presses lower around her pubic area. He takes off his gloves, and writes notes in her chart. Turning around he says to her, "Now Jan, I have to examine your vaginal area, and look inside of it. How hard is your flow today?"

"Today is my last day Doctor, I'm spotting very little, it won't be a big mess," she says with a laugh.

"I am going to get the instrument I need for your exam Jan, the nurse will remain here with you; I will be back in a few moments." He leaves the examination room.

The nurse adjusts her blanket, and pillow, "Are you doing alright Jan?"

"I'll be better when this is over."

He comes back carrying a cloth-covered tray. He sits it down, and washes his hands. The nurse walks over, handing him a clean towel to wipe his hands. He puts on gloves while the she carefully opens the cloth covering the tray.

The nurse tells her "Put your feet into the stirrups Jan and open your legs."

She puts her feet into the stirrups while the nurse holds her gown down.

"I'll go easy Jan, this instrument has been sanitized and warmed up, and it won't be a huge jolt when I insert it."

The nurse pulls her gown back, he leans forward carefully looking around her vaginal area, and then he slowly starts inserting it inside her.

Holding on to the table, she flinches when she feels the warmth starting to enter her.

She thinks to herself "I wonder if the guy I have sex with would be this gentle?"

After a few moments, he pulls it out, placing it back on the tray. The nurse wipes her off, and pulls her gown back down so she is fully covered.

She watches him put several items into an envelope, "I took a swab around your uterus for a pap smear test Jan, I'm sending it to our lab. My nurse will call your mother and tell her when the results are in, then both of you can stop by my office and I will tell you what they are."

"I know about a pap smear test, she already explained it to me Doctor."

"Get dressed Jan, I will be back in a moment."

He leaves the examination room.

She gets up off the table; takes a sanitary napkin, places it in her panties, and pulls them up. The nurse is cleaning up around the sink area, Jan is glad she has not been watching her dressing.

She puts on her pants thinking to herself, "I'm so nervous with that nurse in here, I can only imagine just how I am going to feel when it's a strange man wanting to have sex with me."

She straightens her blouse; The Doctor knocks and enters the examination room just as she sits down.

"I have just a few more questions Jan, we're almost finished here. Everything looked like it should outside and inside. I did not see any abnormal growths on your uterus.

Are you considering having sex anytime soon Jan?"

She feels her face flush in embarrassment, "In my future I might meet a guy I would consider having sex with, but that's a long way off Doctor. We would need to know one another before we did have it."

He writes in her chart, and looks up at her, "You're a virgin Jan, so insist, when that time comes that he goes slow. Also, insist any man you decide to have sex with has had a recent STD test that shows he is clean. Most importantly tell him that he must wear a condom, even if you are taking birth control pills. They don't protect you from getting any sexually transmitted diseases."

Jan smiles at the Doctor, she starts leaving the examination room; "I plan on being very safe Doctor when that time comes. Are you going to tell my mother about our conversation?"

"You're a minor Jan; I suggest that you talk openly with her prior to having sex. She can give you a mother's advice. If you want more information about sex, I have some excellent pamphlets available. If your mother approves, I will be happy to give them to you. I am going to prescribe you birth control and laxatives, both of them should help reduce, or eliminate your cramps, and irregularity. If you have any reaction, or complications, let me know with out delay. The pharmacy will include warnings with your medication. Take the time to read them, and be aware some women do have problems with birth control pills. If you smoke, stop smoking, taking the pill and smoking isn't recommended."

"Thank you Doctor, I don't smoke, nor intend to, and I will read the warnings."

She picks up her prescription slip at the reception desk and leaves the office. Walking to her bus stop, she takes out her cell phone to call home, "You're done at the Doctor's office Jan?"

"Yes, I'm done, the exam was very through, and he gave me two prescriptions to help me. I'm on my way to pick them up; will you please call the pharmacy with your credit card information?"

"I'll do that right after we hang up, there won't be a problem, and I'll see you later at home."

"Bye for now mom, and thanks so much."

She sees the bus coming in the distance. She gets in the bus and sits down. She takes the prescriptions out of her purse to look at them. The Doctor's handwriting is hard to read. She puts them back in her purse, with the thought "With so much education, why can't Doctor's write clearly?"

It does not take her long to get to her stop. She gets off her bus, goes inside, and gives her prescription to the receptionist, "Your mother just called, we have your insurance information. It will be about twenty minutes, you might as well be comfortable," she points at benches nearby.

She walks over and sits down on the bench, "With twenty minutes before they have everything ready, I should get something to drink," she thinks to herself.

She is deep in that thought when a woman walks by, and gives the receptionist her prescription. Jan does not pay attention, until she looks up and sees her walking towards her. Fright fills Jan; she recognizes she is the woman her father is with now! Sitting a few seats away, she notices Jan is looking in her direction. Jan wonders if she saw her when she went to meet her father. Jan starts getting nervous; she discreetly looks at her reading papers the receptionist gave her.

Jan wants to be nosey, but does not want a confrontation either. The receptionist comes back to her desk carrying a bag. "Jan, your prescription is ready now."

The woman looks right at her. She glances away, quickly takes the bag, and runs outside to her bus stop. She steps off the curb hoping she can see if her bus is about to arrive.

Suddenly she hears a voice saying, "Are you Jan, Jack's daughter?"

She turns and looks at her, "I'm his daughter; we haven't met, at least not formally."

"I would like to talk with you, if you will allow me some of your time Jan."

Jan thinks to her self "If I ran right now, I wonder how fast I could get out of here and away from her?"

She sighs and resigns herself to talking with her, "I'm taking the bus home, we can sit in the back and talk.

I had hoped it was here when I came outside."

"I have a car; we can take a drive and talk somewhere near here. If you want me to, I will drop you off by your home, if that is alright?"

Looking around the parking lot, she suspects her father might be somewhere nearby. He could have followed her, and be watching both of them from a distance. Jan feels some relief when she does not see him. She knows the woman senses her being very nervous and angry.

She stands at her bus stop, the woman looks at her. "I won't force you to talk to me Jan, I recognized you, and I thought this might be a good opportunity for both of us to get to know one another a little better."

"Who said that I want to get to know you?"

"I can tell that your angry Jan, I'm only asking you for a little of your time. Maybe I might be able help you in some way?"

"Help me get angrier at you, or my father?"

"It's not my intention to make you angrier Jan. I hope you understand that."

"I have questions, and I need answers, if I ask them, will you give me truthful answers?"

"Yes, Jan, I will, I give you my promise, that, if you will take the time and listen to me, I will tell you the truth that is all I can ask of you."

"Alright I promise to listen to you, what is your name?"

Looking at her, she pauses, "Jan, my name is Irina."

Chapter 6

Jan follows Irina to her car, waiting by the passenger door until she opens it. Jan does not glance at her.

She starts the car, looks into the rear view mirror, and backs out of the parking space.

Jan sits in stunned silence for a moment then says, "I can't say I'm happy to meet you Irina. I saw you at the park after I talked with my father."

"Perhaps what I have to say might help you to not be so angry at me Jan?"

"My mother and I are very angry at you Irina. My father cheated, he left us to be with you."

Irina sees a small park, "Let's takes a walk in that park over there Jan, and is that alright with you?"

"Fine with me, I need fresh air."

She pulls into a parking space they both get out of the car. Jan waits for her to start walking, keeping herself at a distance from her.

"When I first met your father Jan, I was an account executive for a major supplier that sold parts to the business your father works for. I had to deal with him because he ordered what my company was selling."

Jan sees a bench by a tree, "Let's sit there in the shade Irina." Irina follows her and sits down.

She sits away from her. "I have every right to be angry with you Irina; I want you to know that up front." Irina wipes a tear

45

from her face, she looks at her, "I cannot say I blame you Jan, if you want me to finish my story, I'll continue."

"You might as well tell me everything you know Irina. My father certainly isn't willing to do it."

"I met your father over three years ago at his company. We became friends; one time when I was there he asked if I was married, I told him I am a widow. I ask him if he was married, he told me no, he was a widower."

Jan glares at her, "Your lying, Irina, that's a damn lie."

"Jan I didn't ask you to come here with me and lie to you, there has been enough lies."

"Yes, that's the truth, there have been enough lies, I don't have to sit here and listen to yours Irina."

"You told me you had questions, and wanted truthful answers. What ever you ask me, I will tell you the truth

I did not expect to meet you today. I have no idea if your father told you anything about me. I thought if we talked today, you would let me tell you who I really am."

Jan nervously shifts herself on the bench, "Fact is Irina, my mother and I don't know much about you. It was not until we discovered my father was living with you, that we started knowing anything, which was not much. When dad first told mom he wanted a divorce, both of them were ready for it. They drew up papers outlining what they wanted. They read one another's paper and seemed satisfied. Then they gave the papers to an attorney who made it legal. If my father told you he was a widower, how did he explain me to you?"

Irina begins to tense, "Your father told me you were his niece, and your mother was his sister and were taking care of you. It wasn't until earlier this year I accidentally found some papers that revealed to me, you were his daughter."

Jan begins to cry, Irina offers her a tissue, and she takes it, looking at Irina.

"Now do you understand what I said about enough lies?" Irina asks.

"I am trying to grasp some understanding, but what did he tell you when he started living with you, how did he explain my sudden disappearance?"

"Your father told me your mother would care for you. He phrased it "It's best my sister takes care of her.""

"What a web of deceit my father has spun, catching us all in it. I am still am having a hard time believing you Irina, I feel as if you are trying to come between me and my father."

"I'm not trying to become between either of you, when I confronted him about finding his papers by accident, he really became quite angry, accusing me of going through his private and personal papers.

I took him to a desk that we use, opened a drawer and showed him the papers were in plain sight. Since I was looking for papers, he asked me to look for; it was only natural that I would look through them and see if they were what he wanted."

Jan sits staring out into the park, her heart racing, her body shaking.

"I would offer you a hug Jan, but I'm not sure you want one from me?"

Jan looks at Irina, she moves towards her letting her hug, Jan wraps her arms around Irina, both cry.

It takes a few moments to compose themselves.

Jan sits up looking at Irina's face, "I want to believe you Irina. I feel you are being sincere, and telling the truth. It hurts me deeply hearing what you are saying; it is also hurts you telling me. I needed his permission to apply for a job. He said if the job did not affect school, I could work. I asked him to meet and talk with me alone. I told my mother I saw you there. I thought it was his idea having you wait for him while we talked."

"No Jan, It was his idea that I go with him to the park. He said he was going to tell you I just happened to stop by, so he could introduce us."

"Just happened to stop by, as he put it, another damn lie, he wanted to dump on both of us." Jan replies.

"When he came up to me and we started walking out of the park, I asked him if he was going to introduce us. He told me that you got upset and was not ready; I managed to get a glimpse of you. That is how I knew you when I saw you today. I had a lot of apprehension about asking you to talk to me today. I thought you might still be upset, and would not want to talk to me. I have confronted your father more than once about his lies Jan."

"The only way you recognized me was when you saw me meet him? I have given him my school pictures the last three years, with permission from my mother. He has never shown any of them to you?"

"Sorry Jan, no, he hasn't. He told me that he didn't have any of you, that your mother who he referred to as his sister hadn't given him any."

"After listening to what you have told me, no wonder he didn't want us to meet. He knows damn well I would have questioned you. I lit into him about you when we were at the park. He brushed it off by telling me mom and him were immature when they met, and then matured differently and eventually outgrew each other over time."

"I saw you start walking a different direction, but I managed to catch a glimpse of you when he embraced me. I came close to telling your father that you did not look upset. I actually thought you had a smile on your face, or at least it looked like you did."

"Yes, he had agreed I could apply for a job, I was very happy. I had that smile laughing to myself that I managed to chew him out about you, and the divorce. When I told mom about it she reminded me I was lucky dad didn't change his mind."

"Your father has a lot of good qualities, but he has an insecure dark side. It's that side of him that really scares me sometimes."

Jan laughs, "Mom and I thought we were the only ones to see that Irina. I hate to bring it up, but we felt his insecure dark side took over when he started cheating with you."

"I am so very sorry Jan, I hope you know that. I wish I could tell your mother how sorry I am too."

"I accept your apology, it wasn't your fault, like we thought it was Irina. I believe that if you had found out dad was married, you would have never let him get as far as he has. I hope for your sake dad isn't trying to cheat on you too."

"Let's get something to drink from the store over there," Irina says, pointing across from the park.

She moves closer to Irina, holding her hand they walk together. They select their drinks and walk back to the bench where they were sitting.

They sit in silence, and then Jan asks, "What now Irina, we know more by talking with each another today, but what should all of us do about it?"

"I've asked myself a thousand times before Jan, after I've found out he lied to me, what should I do about it? My love for your father keeps blocking my way. Perhaps my wish to be blind and deaf along with my own insecurities keeps me from telling him to go to hell. I often want to hit the road and not look back!"

"For all you know he might be seeing someone that he will eventually replace you with."

"His lie was the grand lie, now I find it very hard to trust him. That is why I believe he asked me to follow him to the park, was to see for myself that he was not meeting another woman. He was meeting you, his daughter, I think he hoped I would start believing he was being truthful, then give him back some of the trust he destroyed."

Jan takes Irina's hand, she holds it looking at her, "Mom sure as hell isn't taking him back, we both know that. He destroyed our trust; he burned all of his bridges behind himself. Have you started suspecting he might be cheating on you too Irina?"

"I don't have positive proof, but I do have my suspicions, especially after he lied to me about you, and your mother. All of his lies are finally coming into play here Jan."

"I'm not going to tell you to try and find out if he is cheating. If that's what you're asking me to do Irina, you'll have to make your own decision."

"I wasn't expecting you to decide for me. Any decision from this point on has to be about myself Jan. I'm very glad you took the time to talk to me, now we both know more facts."

"I'm glad I didn't run away from you I'm sure there is more that none of us know Irina. Dad started his lies three years ago; the truth has finally come out now. He keeps trying to dig out of the hole he dug for himself."

Irina shifts her position on the bench, still holding Jan's hand, "You're a dear sweet girl, despite everything he did to you, and your mother. You have grown and are still growing to be a fine woman Jan, I just wanted to tell you that from my heart."

"I can say truthfully Irina when I first saw you, I wanted so bad to just start running away and not stop until I lost sight of you. I had such anger, and resentment for you. Now that we have talked this afternoon, I feel a calmness I cannot explain. It is as if everything we shared today has finally brought me some peace.

The other day my mother told me that she did not want me to blame myself for their divorce. I told her as a young child I did blame myself for it."

Jan wipes her tears, Irina is also crying. "Oh Jan, no, he would lie, cover up with another lie and another, and another. He caught all of us in a web he has spun. I do not want to go through what your mother has gone through. I hate the idea of finding out another woman has fallen for his lies, just as I did. I don't want anyone else going through the pain all of us have gone through."

She looks at her watch, "I better get you home Jan, I don't want your mother to be worried about you."

"She knows I would be a while at the pharmacy, and getting back home. I want to stay to make sure you have told me everything."

"Your father should have been here too Jan, so he could have listened to both of us, then we could watch his reactions together."

"I won't tell him about meeting you today Irina, or about our conversation. I hope someday he finds the guts to tell my mother and I the real truth, not the lies he has told."

"Will you tell your mother that we met and talked today?"

"I should tell her, I will think about how to tell her on the way home. I have to break it to her easy. When she finds out we met and talked, that will be a shock itself to her."

"Would you like my private office number Jan then you call and ask me anything you might have forgotten or if something comes up?"

She takes her cellular phone out of her purse and puts her number into its memory. "Don't worry Irina, dad doesn't get a copy of my bill, or check who I call."

She offers her number, which Irina writes down on the back of one of her business cards.

"He doesn't see my phone bill either, I get it at my office, and my company pays for it. There isn't any chance of him finding out I have your number, or knowing that you call me."

"Is there anything else you want to tell me before we go?" Jan asks.

Irina is wipes tears from her eyes, she looks at her, "I 'm glad you didn't reject my offer to talk today. Please feel free to call me. I have voice mail in case I am not in the office I am the only one who can access it, leave me a message. I'll get it, and give you a call when I have the chance."

"Only days I can't talk to you are school days, leave me a message, when I get out of class I will call you right back."

She smiles at Jan, "I would like to be your friend Jan, if you want me to be?"

She looks at Irina, "You told me more about things today that I needed to hear. I'm glad I listened to you, friends always tell each other it like it is Irina."

Irina smiles and says, "I don't know any other way Jan. We are very much alike; I also tell my friends it like it is. You needed to vent your anger, which I understand, and you let me vent mine. Friends share good and bad and doing that today allows both of us to leave here a lot less angry then when we first met today."

"We certainly found understanding today Irina. I want to invite you to my birthday. I'm not sure if mom is planning a party, I would like you to stop by anyhow and meet her, if you want to?"

Irina smiles at Jan, "Jan, please tell her we talked and we both came to a peaceful understanding. If she does not want to meet me, I understand, let her know that. I cannot put myself in her shoes, so if she is angry with me and does not want anything to do with me, I would not blame her.

I'm not going to force myself on your mother, or anyone."

She gives Irina's hand a gentle squeeze, "I'll talk to mom Irina; I feel she will at least appreciate knowing what you told me today about dad and what he has been up to. Now I can tell her he is up to no good."

"I'm glad that you talked to me, Jan, we shared a lot today. Thank you for giving me your time, and your feedback."

"Irina, I do have another question for you, why haven't you tried to contact my mother before today and talk to her?"

"Jan, I don't know how mad both of you became when he left her for me, but there is no worse anger than a woman scorned by the man she deeply loves. Do you think she would want to see me on her doorstep telling her what I told you today?"

Jan gives a small giggle, "One good thing is she has never seen you, so she wouldn't know who you were, until you told her."

"I have thought about it, truly, but lost my courage more than once. It took me a lot of courage to run behind you today and even ask you to talk to me Jan."

"I bet you thought I would try to bite your head off, huh?"

"That thought was more like blow my head off with your anger, and I wouldn't have blamed you."

"What if I had gone off and refused to talk to you Irina?"

"All I could have done was to offer my business card with my number and tell you to call me, and then walk away."

They walk to the car, and hug one another tightly.

"Thanks, friend, I appreciate your honesty today. I appreciate your offer to drive me home, but I am going to take the bus. I need time to think."

"Alright Jan, I hope we will be talking again soon." She smiles and drives off.

Chapter 7

Jan sits on the bus as it makes its way towards her home, staring out the window; her mind is spinning from the day's events. Finally, the bus pulls up to the stop near her home, she gets off and begins walking, her thoughts are "What am I going to tell mom about meeting dad's lover, better yet, how am I going to tell her?"

She goes into her home; her mother is still at work. She goes to her room, leaving the door open so she can hear her when she comes home.

She decides her to call Crissy, anxiously waiting for her to answer. Crissy breathlessly answers, "Hello."

"Hi Crissy, do you have time to talk? I had something happen today, and really need to talk to you."

She pauses a moment, "Sure Jan, do you want to talk on the phone or would it be better for you if I come over there?"

"I would appreciate it if you came over Crissy we should talk in person."

"I'll be over in about 15 minutes Jan."

She walks to the living room; and stands by the window until she sees her driving up. She goes outside and waits for her.

Crissy sees the distressed look on her face when she gets out of her car, "Jan, you really look bad, I hope it isn't something the Doctor told you?"

Jan moves fast towards Crissy, she open her arms, both hug not saying anything for a few moments. Jan finally pulls back from her they go into the house.

"Do you want something to drink Crissy?"

"No Jan, tell me what happened, I could feel that you're stressed over the phone. I can see how much now that I'm here."

"First of all Crissy, everything went good at the Doctor's office, he gave me my prescription, which I went to pick up at the pharmacy. While I was waiting at the pharmacy a woman came in, she started to sit down, when I realized she was dad's lover."

Crissy gets a distressed look on her face, she looks at Jan, "Oh my, dear Jan, what a shock!"

Jan smiles as she wipes a tear from her eye, "Crissy, I'm glad you're here before mom gets home, I decided to leave there as fast as I could, but the woman, I now know as Irina followed me and ask me to talk to her."

"Wasn't it being forward and presumptive of her even thinking you would to talk to her?" Crissy asks.

"At that moment I was so angry at her, and how my father left us for her I really didn't want to talk to her. Something inside me said I should at least listen to what she wanted to say to me. The reason I am under a lot of stress, Crissy is I have to tell mom that I talked to her. I do not how she will react.

Thank you for coming over, I needed you to be here with me when I talk to mom."

Crissy moves closer offering her hand. Jan hears her mother's car pulling into the driveway.

They look out the living room window, watching her approach the house. "When she comes in Jan, I will give you whatever support you need to tell her everything, don't hold back anything."

"I need to Crissy; when I tell her that I spent the day talking to my father's lover, no telling what she will do."

Jan stops talking when she hears the door open. Crissy gives her another hug.

Judy walks into the living room, "What a surprise, you must be Crissy, Jan's friend from school? Good to finally meet you, she has been constantly talking about you since school began."

"Nice to meet you too, I've heard a lot of good things about you from her." Crissy says with a smile

Jan says, "Yes mom, this is Crissy, I asked her to come over, and give me her support when I tell you what happened today."

Judy puts down her bags; she walks to the couch, sitting between them, "Did everything go good at the Doctor's?"

Jan's tears begin to fall, she takes a napkin offered by Crissy, "Mom everything went good at the Doctor's. While I was waiting at the pharmacy, a woman came in. She happened to be dad's lover whose name is Irina."

Judy's face reflects the shock and anger she feels, "Did she do something to you Jan, or say something that made you this upset, if so I will confront her about it?"

"Mom, just try to relax and listen, I'm going to make this a short version of what happened. I have debated with myself how to tell you that we spent most of the afternoon talking. "

"Really pisses me off Jan, everything about her," Judy says with anger in her voice.

"I can only fully agree, when I realized who she was I ran out of the pharmacy as fast as I could. She followed and asked me if I would talk to her. Irina told me that she saw me the day I talked to dad. He asked her to come with him because he supposedly wanted to introduce us. However, he chickened out. I know now why he did. He was scared to death I would start asking her questions, and she would answer them truthfully."

"Jan, do you believe Irina, Your father could have told her to lie for him, for all we know. I still find it hard to believe that she was forward enough even asking you to talk to her."

"Oh, I told her I thought she was a liar mom, I tried mentally to block out everything she was saying. A part of me wanted to hear more, so I let her keep on talking. She told me that she met dad at his company three years ago." Jan stops herself while looking at Judy, "Mom, what I'm about to tell you will really make you mad, it did me, are you really ready for this, or do you want me to stop?"

Judy wipes tears from her eyes, "Tell me, Jan, I might as well know everything she had to say."

"Mom, after they became friends, she told him she was a widow, and he told her he was a widower."

Judy angrily jumps up from the couch, "Widower, he told her I was dead?"

"Exactly mom and he told her that you were his sister, and I was his niece."

Judy clinches her fist, her face becomes red from anger, and tears flood her eyes dropping down her face. Jan stands up and hugs her, they both hold on to one another when they feel additional arms: Crissy is hugging them. After a few moments of hugging and silence Judy pulls away, everyone sits back on the couch.

"Are you sure you want me to continue mom?" Jan asks.

"Might as well Jan, please do, we're all sharing this pain together, but at least we have the love and support of your good friend Crissy."

"That's why I called and asked her to stop over, I told her a little before you got home, and she suggested I wait for you."

"I'm glad you did, and thank you Crissy for your support." Judy says.

"Irina told me that she's beginning to distrust dad. She found some papers in their desk that revealed who we really are, his ex wife, and daughter. He got angry with her and assumed she intentionally looked through his private papers. I'm sure he thought they would be hidden from her, but perhaps he forgot about them."

"She didn't think have any reason to distrust or suspect him until after she found those papers mom. I feel she was telling me the truth, as much as I did not want to believe it, I saw it in her face. She said there had been enough lies. Now she thinks he might be lying to another woman. I began to feel relieved of so much pain when she told me all of this. I began to feel a bond between us, she was being honest with me, mom."

"I've got to get a drink; did either of you want anything to drink?" Judy asks

"Just a glass of cold water for me," Jan says.

"I'll take a glass of cold water too, if you don't mind." Crissy replies.

Judy goes into the kitchen to get the water.

Crissy looks at Jan, "I'm proud of your strength and courage telling your mother what Irina told you Jan."

"Not easy Crissy, not easy at all, but I feel much better after telling her. I hope she starts feeling better too. It's been too long for both of us to even feel good about anything."

Crissy gives her a hug.

Judy sits the glasses of water in front of them. "Thank you Jan, for telling me everything, it hurts both of us. We will find a way to grow, and be stronger by knowing everything she told you today."

Judy takes a drink. Sitting down her glass, "Liar, your father has done nothing but lie to us the past three years.

Part of me wants to confront him about this, but another part of me is finally at peace that the truth came out, no matter what the source.

Truth hurts Jan, your father doesn't feel comfortable telling either of us the truth."

"Doesn't he realize or even know that eventually we would find out mom, that's what's bothering me, the most."

Judy sits back on the couch offering her hands to Jan and Crissy. "Jan, your father has lied for so long, I would bet he has started believing his lies are the truth."

Crissy leans forward, "Can I say something here, if you don't mind?"

Jan and Judy look at Crissy, "Of course you can say something Crissy. You're a friend here for Jan, and supporting me too, I'm very grateful for it."

Crissy smiles, "My father lied to my mother and I too, we knew it right off but we didn't let him know we saw through them. We wanted to see just how far he would go. After a while when we got together with him, we told him we knew he was lying, so he might as well tell us himself what the truth was."

Judy looks at her, "Did your father cheat on your mother Crissy? I shouldn't be so nosy, I'm sorry, that just came out."

"It's ok, your not nosy, my father did cheat, with not just one woman; there were several women he was cheating with. Certainly not the circumstances you have had here, he began working late, going in early, suddenly working weekends."

Judy and Jan look at one another seeing the shock in each other's face.

Jan looks at her, "What did you two do when you saw that?"

"You're going to love this, soon we both began to suspect him, so we followed him and saw him meet a woman at a restaurant, and they went inside and sat together. We let them get very comfortable, and then we both walked in. You should have seen the look on his face when saw both of us walking to their table." Crissy says with a laugh in her voice.

"My mother puts her hand towards the woman not even looking at him and says, Hello, I hope your enjoying my husband, and will continue to enjoy him. I'm divorcing him for cheating with you.

The woman was shocked, but shook her hand.

Mom looked her right in the face and says, "Honey, we have been following and watching him meet his ladies. You might think you're the only one, but your just one of several or more women we have seen him with: we didn't get the chance to introduce ourselves to the others." Crissy wipes a tear from her face and begins to laugh.

Jan and Judy try to muffle their laughs, but cannot contain their feelings seeing in their minds the event she described.

"What a scene, I can only imagine his face when he saw both of you there. No telling what he thought when your mother just came out and said that." Jan says with a laugh.

"She got up, looked at him, took her glass of water, threw it in his face and walked out in disgust."

Judy slowly stops laughing, "That was quite a story Crissy, thank you for sharing it; we all needed a good laugh today. What else did you and Irina talk about Jan?"

"We talked about how he has spun his web of deceit. Sad thing is he put himself in it, not us. She gave me her work number to call if there are any questions I might have. I gave her my number so she can call me too. Before she left, I called her friend, I consider her not just my friend, but also our friend mom. It was very hard for her to tell me how they met. She apologized because of what dad did to both of us.

She is very sad that he could be starting to cheat on her."

"She certainly came across as a friend who wanted to share her secrets, pains and not get herself caught up any further in his lies. I have to ask you Jan, was she a pretty lady?"

"I would call her plain, not a lot of makeup, just lipstick, her hair was dark brown, long, and she had it pulled back behind her head. She had on a business suit, but instead of pants, she had a dress that came up just above her knees."

"I had to ask, I feel better that she wasn't a model." Judy says

"I told Irina I want her to come if I'm having a birthday party, Is it alright that I asked her mom?"

"Oh Jan, part of me is still mad as hell at her, another part of me wants to meet her. I think I would feel better having her personally apologize to me."

"Irina said she wouldn't come if it was too uncomfortable for you mom."

"She made an effort to be a friend Jan, if we have a birthday party for you, she can come."

"Thank you mom," Jan replies.

"Really sad, that both our fathers chose to do this to all of us without thinking about the affects it would have on all our lives." Crissy says.

"We all find a way to go on Crissy; nothing can change the past, only what we do today will change the many tomorrows we have ahead of us."

"Jan thanks for asking me to be here, I hope I've been some support, by hearing what your father did; what Irina told you has also given me some peace too."

"Life goes on Crissy, your life, our life, your father's life, and Jack's life. I am sad to say those men will look back and see what they missed, what they chose to abandon, and want it all back. The reality will hit them that isn't possible, what's gone, is gone forever."

Crissy looks at her watch, "I have to go now, but if you need more backup, I want you both to know that I'm offering mine in case you want to confront Jack."

"No, I'm not going to confront him, I feel sooner or later Irina will tell him about meeting Jan. Let her tell him we know about his lies. Maybe he will come to both of us either telling more lies, or the real truth."

Jan, Judy and Crissy share one more group hug; they walk her to the door. She walks to her car, opens her door, waves, and leaves.

"What a day Jan, lets eat, help me with dinner."

"Thank you for being my best friend mom."

Chapter 8

Jan tries to chase sleep out of her mind; her waking thoughts are on her birthday one week away. She tries to focus getting ready for school. Gathering her books, she makes sure her assignments are in her backpack. When she walks into the kitchen, she does not see Judy.

She picks up a note on the table, "Jan, I went to work early today, I will be home when you get home from school, love mom"

Jan decides to drink apple juice; maybe she will eat something at school. She leaves her house, getting to her bus stop just as it pulls up, getting on she starts walking to the back when she sees a familiar face, Mary.

She decides she will sit next to her. "Hi Mary, It's been a while since we last saw each other."

She looks at her, "Hello Jan, nice to see you again too."

They sit silently as the bus makes its way through traffic; they get off together at school. "Can I talk with you a few moments before class Mary?" Jan asks.

Mary glances at her watch, she looks at her "If you want to know why I went back to work Jan, I have my reasons."

"Crissy told me all about the job, you returned before I could start working Mary. I was not even thinking about asking you why you went back. All I wanted to ask you, is if your planning to work longer than you previously did?"

She looks around making sure no one is nearby. They start walking towards an open area on the school grounds. "Jan, like both of you I know I will need college to succeed; I can't say for sure how long I will keep working. Probably when I have made enough to pay for another two years, but I can't tell you when that might be. I quit when I finally had thirty thousand saved up, it was enough to pay the first two years of college, and I needed time off too."

"Thirty thousand dollars, damn, that's a lot for just working weekends only." Jan says with surprise in her voice.

"Correct, Jan, thankfully the guy I first met was more than generous, Nick is really great too. I am finished with this work after I accomplish my goal. You'll find out yourself, it's very draining, even doing it one day a week Jan."

"Crissy has already explained that to me Mary; I didn't imagine letting a guy use my body for money would be a piece of cake."

"Not even Jan, I've worked even if I didn't feel good. There have been times where I have literally forced myself to act. You become a sex actor, and the better sex act you do will have him putting more money in your hand."

"Please don't get the impression that I'm asking you to stop working just because of my needs Mary."

"Crissy already told me that your seventeen, so Mr. Junkett won't even consider talking to you until after your eighteen."

"I know that Mary, my birthday is almost here. I understand why you have returned to work. I'll wait until you decide to stop being an escort."

They start walking towards their classes when she sees Crissy walking their way, "There's Crissy Mary."

"Good morning, I see you two meet again, anything discussed I can add too?"

Mary smiles at her, she takes Jan's hand, "We met on the bus today; and have talked. We have a better understanding about why I returned to work."

"Jan doesn't hold a grudge Mary; over the past few days I have seen a side of her that has really inspired me."

"I didn't think she had a grudge, she had concerns. We both talked about both of ours Crissy. Time to get to class, Jan I hope we can become better friends."

"I appreciate that Mary," Jan says, all three girls hug one another.

Jan and Crissy start walking to their class, "I made it clear to her that I wasn't mad she returned to work Crissy."

"She probably wants to make enough to pay for another two years of college Jan."

"She told me that, I can't blame her, if it had been me, I would want to do exactly the same."

"College isn't cheap, it gets more expensive each year Jan. Even though Nick is very generous, I still worry about being able to afford four years of college. I have even considered trying to find more work, that way I can quit too, and soon."

"Mary mentioned to me how it affects her Crissy, just like it has you."

"Imagine Jan, you don't feel up to it, you will hope it ends fast, so you can take his money and run."

"I've never had sex, I've only heard a lot about it from other girls who said they love it, of course they are not escorts either, and Mary said she often felt like a sex actor."

"Keep in mind those girls brag they love it because it keeps their guy hanging around. When they stop putting out, he finds another girl who will."

"I don't want to just put out to keep a guy hanging around with me. I would rather develop some feelings, and hope he does too, Crissy."

"If she leaves Jan, and you work with me, prepare yourself to have no feelings; just make money, a lot of it. The guys are married; you don't want to get attached to them."

"I agree Crissy, but doesn't Nick care about you, with some feelings?"

"I put out Jan, his wife doesn't, he knows his money buys pleasure those are the feelings he has for me."

Jan shakes her head, she feels disturbed after hearing what Crissy said to her. They go to class, take tests and turn in their assignments.

"Have you thought some more about your dad, and Irina Jan?"

"My minds still spinning after meeting her, and talking to mom Crissy, I hope he will start feeling guilty enough to talk to both of us. I've prepared myself in case he doesn't want to."

"He might Jan, my father finally talked to my mother, a lot of years after their divorce. Would you like to have lunch with me?"

"I'll pass, I didn't have breakfast, and I don't really feel like eating at the moment Crissy."

They walk to the bus stop together; "You know I have your back if you need support Jan. I'm there for you if you don't want to go alone and talk to your dad."

"Mom and I decided both of us will do it together, neither one of us wants to be alone with him when we talk to him."

Jan and Crissy hug, Jan closes her eyes until the bus pulls up to her stop near her home.

When she walks into her house, Judy is sitting on the couch with tears in her eyes; "Mom, what happened?"

"Sit down Jan; I'm afraid I have bad news."

Jan drops her backpack; she walks over and sits next to her, "Irina followed your father today, she saw him meeting and talking with a woman. She decided to confront them; she finds out the woman also met him at his work. He had given her the same story, he was a widower."

"What did she do mom?"

"She did what any of us would do; she told her the story about all of us. She told her he was nothing but a liar, then she told him had to move out of her house, immediately."

"So she told her in front of dad, that she met me, and what we talked about?"

"She also told him exactly what you told each other."

Judy composes herself, "He called me right after she lit into him and demanded that I should tell him what I knew. I told him that I didn't have to tell him a damn thing about you meeting her. His lies and now this other woman, that was the last straw for her, she wants nothing more to do with him."

"Did he think I made her tell me he was a liar, and a cheater?" Jan says with sarcasm in her voice.

"Jan, he started cursing me and calling me names, I held the phone away while he was screaming into my ear, finally I hung up on him. Irina calls right after he did, telling me he was packing up his belongings and moving out. She wanted to warn me, he was leaving. She asked me if I thought he might come over here."

"Wow, what did you tell her mom?"

"I told her I had no idea where your father was going, all I know is he will not dare come here."

'As paranoid as dad sounds, he might think all of us have started conspiring against him." Jan says looking at Judy.

"As far as any conspiracy, your father should know he created his own."

They sit looking at one another, the phone rings.

They both stare at the phone; Judy answers, "Jack, before you start in on me, I need to say something I should have said a long time ago."

She puts her hand over the phone, "Jan, run to your room and listen in on your extension."

She runs to her room, and picks up her phone.

"What do you want to say now Jack? I hung up on you earlier because of your foul language and failing to listen to anything I had to say."

After a pause, he says, "Judy, I'm really sorry about my language, I lied, you know that, as well as myself, and I've hurt you, and hurt Jan. Because of those lies I've lost a woman I really cared for."

Judy restrains her anger, "You don't think your lies and our loss was relevant Jack? You are failing to understand you have two women here, who you should have cared more for. You decided to lie about us being your sister, and niece. You didn't even think about us when you told those lies, did you Jack?"

After a pause, he says, "Judy, I'm sorry, I really do regret the lies, they have all caught up with me. I need therapy or counseling to help me understand why I have hurt so many of you."

"You're now aware that Irina told Jan she suspected you Jack. You had to be very stupid not realizing all of us women are smart and would eventually catch you in your lies?"

"Yes, I'm aware, she told me everything today, and how she acted, and showed maturity beyond her years."

"Something she obtained on her own Jack, despite you, or what you did or didn't do. She was really hurt Jack, you didn't even think how the hurt would affect us?"

"No use to rehash old things Judy, we could go over and over it, and nothing would make sense. It doesn't even make sense to me."

"The therapy you mentioned Jack, it might help you to sort things out. I want to wish you well, if you do go and just be honest to your therapist about yourself first."

Jack pauses a moment, "I'm moving, I'll be staying in the city, for a week in a motel or hotel that rents by the week. I'll decide where to move on a permanent basis, when things get better."

"Don't be calling me Jack, or calling Jan, don't take your anger out on us, you brought all this on yourself."

"I thought about asking if I could stop by tonight Judy, that's not the best of ideas, so rest assured I would call and ask you if I could stop by."

"We do not need you to stop by Jack; it is not what we want. Irina had already called and told us that you were mad. She offered to be here if we needed her. I'm more than glad she took her time and talked to Jan, it certainly cleared up a lot for us Jack."

"I should have done a lot of things differently Judy, but I didn't, and again I'm very sorry for both of your pain."

"Jan has been listening in on our conversation Jack, why don't you tell her yourself?"

He pauses a moment, "Jan, I'm sorry, I cannot make up enough to you, I hope you know I'm truly sorry."

Jan composes herself, "First dad, I appreciate you giving me permission to work. With both of you on the phone, a girl took her job back at Mr. Junkett's. Another thing dad is I am disappointed with how you have acted. I'm hurt, and it will eventually go away dad, but not the memory of it, please go and get the help you need."

"I really don't know what else to say; besides I'm really sorry. About the job Jan, maybe she won't last and you can always look for another job."

"I plan on looking dad, right now, please pay mom on time. When I start working, whenever that might be, I'll take care of my own expenses."

"Why you were at the pharmacy in the first place Jan?" He asks.

Judy interrupts, "That's none of your business, Jack, so why did you even ask her that?"

"Because I'm still her father, if there is something medically wrong, I should know, that's why Judy."

"Mom, dad, please, let's stop arguing, we're all stressed out enough as it is."

"Your right Jan, I didn't think I was starting any argument, it came across that way. I need to get out of here; she is getting anxious for me to leave. Jan, please let me know if you find work, I hope you know I'll be there for you if you need me."

"I'll be fine dad; I learned a long time ago, how to take care of myself, thank you any ways." She says with hurt in her voice.

"Jack, get help, get it soon, and prove to her you can be the father she needs."

"I know Judy, and I'm sorry, I must go now."

Jan comes out of her room; she walks to the living room,

"I'm going to call Crissy mom, she offered to stop by and help us if dad came over. I need to let her know everything is alright."

"Crissy is a true friend Jan and if we need her, Irina will be there for us too."

Jan pauses before walking back to her room she looks at Judy. "I can't help but wonder what dad might have in mind for my birthday?"

"We can have a quiet birthday celebration Jan, if you want, all this has causes us so much stress. Neither of us wants any more. I believe your father will probably prefer to meet you alone and give you your present. I'm sure he suspects everyone might be here, and wants to avoid a scene as much as I do."

Jan smiles at Judy, "You really don't have to plan a party mom, and you need your rest to."

"We have several days before your big event Jan, we will talk more about it later."

"Fine mom, I'm going to my room and call Crissy, good night, and I love you."

"Love you too Jan, I'm really proud of you."

Jan goes into her room, she dials Crissy's number, "Crissy, it's Jan, I wanted to let you know everything is alright here, how about you?"

"Everything here is good too Jan, I'll talk to you more tomorrow, I'm busy washing my gym clothes, right now."

"Oh, I didn't mean to interrupt you Crissy, we survived dad calling us."

"See if you can get to school a little early, we will talk before class Jan, is that alright?"

"Well, yes, sure Crissy, Will I see you tomorrow at the school bus stop?"

"Yes, Jan, we will talk then, good night."

Jan hangs up feeling depressed that she was abrupt and did not seem interested in listening to what happened. She takes her bath, washes her hair, puts her nightgown on, lays on her bed in the darkness, and thinks to herself "Something must not be right, Crissy doesn't usually act that way."

Chapter 9

Jan sees Judy sitting at the breakfast table.

"Doing alright this morning mom?"

"I'm getting there, last night I had eight hours of rest. I scrambled eggs this morning, help yourself." Jan sits and eats, when finished, she says, "We'll be fine mom, please try to not worry."

She smiles, looks at her watch, "I'll see you when you get home this afternoon Jan."

Jan picks up her backpack, "I love you mom, and I'll see you later."

Crissy is waiting for her when she gets school. They hug then begin to walk "I can't help but wonder Crissy, is everything alright, last night you came across a little abrupt."

"Sorry Jan, mom and dad had a major argument on the phone, mom got upset; she didn't want to talk about it. You called at a bad time for both of us, I should have said something, but mom was standing near me, she thought it was my dad calling again."

"I understand now Crissy, I hope that isn't something which will affect you, or your work."

"I'm tough Jan, mom and dad have their differences now and then, I deal with it."

"Crissy I've made up my mind I'm going to start looking for work, even if it's minimum wage, that's better than nothing at this point."

"Do you have any idea what kind of work your going to look for Jan?"

"No Crissy, after my birthday, I'll go to the unemployment office and get advice from them."

"They should help you Jan, take your resume with you. Have someone look at it to help you find something you are qualified to do. "

"Anyhow, I am not upset Crissy, just very concerned. You did not act like yourself. I know when mom and dad had their arguments before they divorced it affected me. "

"I'm glad your not too upset Jan, I wish we could work together, we have a good friendship this year. I'm thankful it's finally our senior year."

I am glad we made it this far Crissy; we will make it all the way. There is nothing I can do about what Mary decides Crissy, it's her choice, I have to respect that."

"Mary is her own person Jan, I can't do anything either about her decision. I haven't talked to Mr. Junkett, so I can't say how he feels about it."

"I'm sure if his clients are happy, then he is happy Crissy. It's all about money anyhow; he probably gets some sort of kickback from the men, since he provides the girls for them."

"We have just a few moments after class, lets wait until we're done then you can tell me about yesterday Jan."

They enjoy gym class; after it ends, they begin walking across the field. "Do you feel like telling me about what happened to your father?"

Jan stops walking, "Let's sit down Crissy." They sit on the grass she looks at her. "Dad called and told mom how sorry he was about all of his lies.

He tried to give her a guilt trip about having to leave because Irina caught him cheating, and lying to her."

"I figured you and your mother were alright when you didn't call me Jan.

I know it wasn't easy for either of you."

"I'm just worried about what dad has in mind for my birthday." Jan says.

Crissy reaches for her hand, "A big step Jan, eighteen, tomorrow is your day. The age when you can finally start making your own decisions, the day you become independent in many ways. Try not to worry about it Jan, I would bet he wouldn't show up, especially after everything that's happened."

"Mom said the same thing Crissy, so I'm not going to worry, I'm just going to enjoy the moment tomorrow."

Crissy walks away leaving Jan to wait for her bus, Jan watches her disappear across the field. She looks towards the sky and feels the warmth of the sun. Her thoughts are "I just want peace, love and contentment, if there is a birthday wish I could have, I really wish for that."

She knows winds of change are upon her, she has a fleeting thought, "Where will those winds take me and what will happen when they do?"

When she gets home, she briefly says hello to Judy, then goes to her room to complete homework.

She is excited her birthday is finally here, but has a sadness that she is not making the money Crissy and Mary make.

She walks out of her room, "Mom, I'm going to bed early tonight, I don't need the stress to affect my studies."

"A long rest is good for you Jan; I'll talk to you in the morning."

Friday morning, "Eight am," she thinks to herself. She prepares herself for the day. Looking around her room, she sees her toys, dolls, little things she has collected over the years.

She looks at her reflection in the mirror admiring her shape, and figure thinking to herself "Eighteen, I'm finally here, now to finish my last year of school."

She is combing her hair when she hears a knock at her door, "Jan, can I come in?"

"Come in mom, I'm just combing my hair".

Judy opens the door to her room, she has a present in her hand "Jan, I wanted to be the first to say, happy birthday to you." She hands her the present, and gives her a big hug.

"Thanks so much mom, you didn't have to get me anything, just the fact you love me so much is the best present in the world." She carefully opens her present and finds a photo brooch inside; she opens it and there is a photo of herself on one side and Judy on the other side.

Engraved inside, "Happy eighteen Jan, love mom."

"Its beautiful mom," She takes it and puts it around her neck. She admires the brooch in her mirror Judy stands behind her smiling. The phone suddenly rings startling both of them.

"I'll answer it mom."

She hears Jack's voice saying "Happy birthday Jan."

"Thanks dad, so far I'm having a happy birthday."

She looks at Judy who goes to her room and picks up her phone.

"Are you there Jan?"

"I was almost finished getting ready when you called; I had to put things down so I can talk to you."

"Don't worry I'm not going to barge in on your special day Jan, but I have a special present I want to give you, if you will meet me?"

She pauses, "Mom didn't say if she had even planned anything dad, like a party, I think we're just going to quietly celebrate together, but where did you want to meet?"

"If your mother doesn't mind, I'll drive by the house; park across the street, then you can come outside and get your present."

Judy cannot restrain herself and says, "I'm listening in on the other line Jack, I do mind, Jan I want you to feel safe meeting your father, what's your choice?"

"I'll go over to Crissy's house, if that's alright with her, and meet you there dad. I need to call her first and ask her if that will be alright."

"Call me back and let me know Jan, it isn't my intention to disrupt your very special day."

"I'll get back to you as soon as I can dad."

Judy walks back into her room; "I'll see if I can get a hold of Crissy mom, don't worry, I plan on being very safe around him."

She calls Crissy, "Crissy, can I ask you for a big favor?"

"Sure Jan, what can I do for you, oh, and happy birthday."

"Thanks Crissy, the reason I called is that dad wants to meet me and give me his present. Mom doesn't want him coming by our house, would it be alright if I meet him over by yours?

He will meet me outside; you can be there to back me up so he will not try to pull anything."

"Of course you can do that, I'll ask my mom to be with us too, about what time were you thinking?"

"How about within the hour, all I have to do is call him, by the time I get to your house; he should arrive right after I get there."

"Perfect, mom's listening to me talking to you, she nods in agreement that it's safest for us to be here with you. We'll see you in about an hour."

She calls him, "Dad, meet me outside of Crissy's house I should be there within the hour."

"Alright birthday girl, I'll see you there."

She walks out of her room, Judy's in the kitchen, "I'm going to meet dad outside Crissy's house."

"I'll see you when you get home, keep your cell handy in case he tries pulls anything, don't be afraid to call 911 Jan."

"If he becomes a problem I will mom,"

She arrives at Crissy's house, and sees her waiting outside. "I can't tell you how thankful I am that both of you are willing to help me out Crissy."

She looks up and down the block. Crissy takes her hand, "We'll watch for him from our window Jan, lets go inside."

Crissy's mother, Kathy says "Happy birthday Jan," and gives her a present. She feels the tears filling her eyes, "I didn't expect either of you to get me anything, your love and friendship is my greatest gift."

"Sit on the couch, and open your present Jan, I'll watch for your father." Crissy says.

When she lifts, the lid of the box there is a beautiful dress inside. She pulls it out and stands up putting it next to herself to see how it fits.

"You certainly will look beautiful in that when you start working." Crissy says.

"How did you know my size?" She asks looking at Crissy with a puzzled look on her face.

"Crissy smiles at her and says "Forgive me, but I snuck a look when we were at gym class Jan."

"Go try it on Jan, let us see how you look in it." Kathy says.

She goes to the bathroom and puts on her new dress. She looks at herself in the bathroom mirror it fits her perfectly.

She thinks to herself "Any man, who sees me in this, would want to spend thousands on me."

A knock on the door startles her; "I saw your dad coming up the block, he'll be outside in a second."

Jan picks up her other clothes and quickly walks to the window. He is parking across the street.

Crissy and her mother stand besides her looking outside, "You look beautiful, go out there, be strong, we're with you all the way."

Jan smiles, straightens her dress, opens the door, she walks to his car. He watches her crossing the street; with a big smile on his face.

He rolls down his windows, "Happy birthday Jan you certainly look beautiful in that dress." He looks behind her and sees Crissy and her mother watching them from the curb, "I notice that you have some backup Jan."

"My trust issues with you dad, your going to have to work for my trust for a long time, and thank you for the compliment," she walks around the front of his car, to the passenger side; he has already opened the door for her.

Pausing, she gives Crissy and her mother a smile and nod, and then she opens the door sitting down with her feet on the asphalt. She looks at Crissy and Kathy who are keeping a watchful eye on her. He hands her his present and she opens it taking a beautiful watch out of its box. She admires the shine of its metal, and its fresh new look. She makes sure they can see what she's doing from across the street both of them smile.

"Its beautiful dad and looks very expensive, I can certainly use a new watch." She says looking at the worn out one on her wrist.

"Look on the back of it Jan." He says.

Engraved on the watches back is "Happy 18, love dad."

She reaches over and gives him a hug and a kiss. She sits back seeing a tear falling from his eye.

"Great dress Jan, was it a gift, from your friends over there?" He says looking at them.

"Yes, something I can wear when I start looking for a job dad. Bye for now dad, thank you for the watch, I'll be calling when I find that job."

She waits until drives away; then she walks over to them with a smile.

"We're glad everything went alright between you and him Jan, we were ready just in case." Crissy says.

"What a great watch Jan." Kathy says as she takes Jan's arm to look at it.

"This certainly has been a wonderful day thanks to both of you.

I should get back home and show mom my great dress, and new watch."

"We will be in touch later Jan," Crissy says while giving her a hug.

She takes the ride back to her home. When she gets off the bus, she sees Judy outside of the house with a bundle in her arms. "Need any help with that mom?"

"Oh Jan, what a wonderful dress, your home already, I hope everything went well with your father?"

"Crissy and her mother gave me the dress mom, isn't it beautiful? Dad gave me this watch, which I certainly can use. He was on his best behavior, probably because he saw them ready to back me up."

"What are you going to do with your old watch Jan?"

At that moment, Jan sees Mrs. James, one of their elderly neighbors walking down their street.

She walks towards her, "Hello Mrs. James, I don't know you that well, I'm Jan, and we see each another once in a while, I would like you to have this," she gives her old watch to her.

She looks at her, "How did you know I needed a watch? This is wonderful, I certainly appreciate that Jan." They hug one another then she watches her walk back to her home carefully putting the watch on admiring it.

"How generous Jan, I can't say enough how proud I am to be your mother. You're a wonderful daughter, now let's go inside."

She sees the bundle that Judy was holding near the door, "What about this mom?"

"Leave it there, Jan, I'll take care of it later."

She goes to the window "Isn't it funny, that old watch, I thought of it as totally useless, but Mrs. James accepted it as if it were brand new."

Judy walks over and puts her arm around her waist, "It was the thought Jan, you thought of her. She accepted your old watch, it was new to her, because it was something she didn't have, but does now, because of your generosity."

Judy walks to the kitchen, "I'm glad your father was well behaved"

"Better than I expected, I reminded him about trust he needs to work on with me. I didn't mention you mom, but I made my point."

Judy gets a smirk on her face when she looks at Jan, "Seems we're both in competition to make our points. I do hope one day your father understands just what our point is."

She goes back outside, she brings the bundle in, setting it behind the couch, she looks at Jan, "Why don't you take a nap, I have some things to finish up here Jan."

"I can use a nap, mom, wake me around two if it isn't too much trouble." Jan says.

"Two it is Jan, I'll be quiet so you can rest." Judy smiles at Jan who is walking towards her room.

Jan lays her dress over a chair she lies down on her bed. Her mind is restless, so much in a short time. She wants to dream of June, when she graduates; she wants to dream about college. She has so many dreams, all she can do is hope one of them will come true. She plays with her necklace, looking at her watch. Two different items, one from her mother, the other from her father, she takes her watch off, reading the inscription on its back. "It's says almost exactly the same thing mom had inscribed on my brooch," she thinks to herself. She finds it hard to understand how two people could love each other so much, and then end up hating each other so much. She closes her eyes wishing she could see her future, the man she will eventually meet. The children she will have. She hopes someday her children will not be lying in their beds, having their minds thinking like she is now.

Chapter 10

Jan hears a knock on her door, she looks at her watch; it is four pm.

"I got busy Jan, I'm sorry to wake you up late, come out as soon as you can."

"I needed the rest mom; I'm not mad, I'll take a shower, and be there as soon as I can."

She gets out of bed, takes her shower washes her hair. She sits at her bureau looking in the mirror, thinking to herself "I don't look older, thank goodness, but I'm sure happy I'm finally eighteen."

She finishes fixing her hair, puts her dress, and makeup on.

She starts walking to the living room, before she gets there; she hears voices saying in unison, "Surprise, happy birthday Jan."

She walks into the living room and sees Crissy, her mother Laura, Mary, Irina, Judy, several aunts and uncles.

"Wow, thanks everyone." She says with a huge smile on her face.

She looks at the dining room table; on it are presents, a large cake with eighteen candles. Above the table is a large banner across the entire room, "Happy Eighteenth Birthday, Jan."

"I know now that's what you had under your arm when I came home today mom."

Everyone surges forward hugging her, giving her a kiss, telling her happy birthday.

"So wonderful to have all the very special people in my life here, I really wasn't expecting a party, thanks so much. A very warm hello to Irina, a new friend," Jan says wiping tears out of her eyes.

"Everyone is waiting for you to open your presents Jan." Judy says.

She picks up the closest present, opening its card, "Happy birthday Jan, love Irina."

Jan removes wrapping off the box. She holds up a silver bracelet to show everyone. "Thank you so much Irina, it's so beautiful."

Irina smiles and winks at her, "You're so very welcome Jan, I'm happy you like it."

Jan opens a card on top of a small box, "My love always, your friend Crissy. She opens the box, inside is a half heart pendant on a chain.

She proudly shows it to everyone. "Oh Crissy, it's wonderful, half of your heart for me, and yes you have the other half of my heart, and always will."

Jan takes another present, reading its card "Happy birthday Jan, love Aunt Linn.

"Aunt Linn thanks so much," she opens a box containing earrings and puts them in her ears letting everyone see them. She finishes opening presents. She talks individually with each person who gave her one.

"Everyone here is my present that I don't have to open; I appreciate all of you, especially all the love you give me."

Mary walks up to her and hands her an envelope, she opens it and sees a hundred dollar bill inside.

"I didn't expect you to be here Mary; or expect you to give me a gift. It's more than generous, thank you."

"It's only a little out of what I have make, Jan. I wanted to show you how very well work pays. "

Jan holds the envelope; she looks around making sure no one is listening, "It's not nice of you to tease me Mary. I can only hope it will be real soon that I'm working too."

Judy calls Jan, "Come and blow out your candles, and make your birthday wish."

Everyone around the table sings happy birthday. Jan closes her eyes.

She blows her candles out. "I just wish for eighteen more years."

She cuts a small piece of cake, "The rest is yours, everyone."

Judy and Jan make sure everyone gets a piece of cake.

Judy sees Mary across the room, "I don't know her, does she go to school with you Jan?"

"That's Mary mom, Mr. Junkett hired her back, and she took the job I asked you and dad if I could apply for."

Judy looks at her, then Jan, "You'll find something, who could resist you Jan, the way you look now?"

Everyone finishes eating and talking with Judy, and Jan. One by one, they begin to leave.

Crissy, Laura, and Irina help Judy clean up, washing dishes, putting things away.

When, everyone is finished. Jan hugs Irina, Laura, and finally Crissy.

Crissy whispers in Jan's ear "Call me later; I'll share more information with you I can't now."

"I'll call you just before I go to bed Crissy."

Jan and Judy walk everyone to the door, watching them leave.

They walk back in the living room, she looks at Jan, "Certainly was a great party Jan, I'm glad you were surprised. I saw Mary give you an envelope but you didn't show anyone what she gave you."

She takes the envelope out of her dress pocket, "Would you believe she gave me a hundred dollars mom. She more or less was bragging how much she earned working where I should be working."

Judy looks at her, "What nerve she has, rubbing her money in your face Jan. Did she come with Crissy?"

Jan's face gets red, as she feels angry.

She takes a deep breath, "I want to be mad as hell about her gift of money. However, I refuse to be mad, especially, on my birthday! I'll ask Crissy if she came with her."

"Thinking about work Jan, have you looked for or thought of any that you could apply for until another job with Mr. Junkett becomes available?"

"Not really, I plan on looking in the paper, go to the unemployment office and see if they have any jobs that haven't been in the paper. I am going to lay down again mom despite my nap I am still tired. I'll call Crissy and thank her again for my dress, and the wonderful half heart pendant."

"Again happy birthday Jan, I'm so happy I was able to surprise you, go rest, we'll talk more in the morning."

Jan goes to her room, she calls Crissy, "Great party Jan, I am so happy you love the heart."

"I sure do Crissy; you said you had more to tell me, what's on your mind?"

"Is your mom nearby Jan?

"Hold on Crissy, let me go look."

She lays her phone down; opens her door and walks to the living room. Judy is busy working on papers she has laid out on the dining room table.

She returns to her room, picking up her phone, "No, she's busy finishing papers she brought home from work Crissy."

"I'm sorry about what Mary did Jan, that really wasn't necessary."

Jan stays silent a moment, she knows she did not show Crissy the envelope, or what was in it.

"I don't understand Crissy; do you mean her coming to my party?"

"She knew your birthday was coming up, you had told her Jan. Your mother had talked to mine; she told her she was planning a surprise party for you."

"You didn't bring her with you, did you Crissy?"

"Mary asked me if you were going to have a party, could she could come. I did not think if she did, it would be a problem. She obviously decided to come by her self. Then yesterday she calls me and said instead of a present she was thinking about giving you a hundred dollars. I told her that was not a good idea. Someone might see her giving you money, and wonder how your girl friend came up with that much money for you. Neither of us can risk anyone finding out we're escorts."

Jan interrupts Crissy, "When she gave the envelope to me, I suspected it was money Crissy. I made sure no one saw what she did. I was not about to say a thing about her gift like I did others; I was shocked she was bold enough to do that at my party. I felt she was trying to make me jealous. Why do you think she would do that? What you two make should be considered personal and private, and be bragging rights."

"Mary is strange, we both saw that today, to her, money is power, I believe she enjoys showing its power to others who don't have it."

"I can use the money; I don't need her to rub it in my face Crissy."

"What I wanted to tell you is something she shared with me. She has begun working with an escort agency. Men call the agency, select certain ages, types of woman. If she fits his description, the agency gives her the job. Thing is, she pays a driver, pays the agency, so she has to really fleece the client for as much cash as she can get. I cannot understand her doing that; she talked Mr.

Junkett into letting her go back to Nick because he was so very generous."

"Sounds like our girl Mary is getting greedy Crissy. Is Mr. Junkett aware of this?"

"Not to my knowledge, besides if he finds out she started working for an agency, I know he would not let her work for him."

"Doesn't sound to me like she will be able to stay with him if she keeps that up," Jan says.

"She wants the money, pure and simple, as fast as she can get it. She has gotten greedy, and greed can become addictive, especially when it comes to money. I wanted to suggest if she approaches you about working for any agency, do not do it Jan. You could end up wearing yourself out real fast trying to get more and more money out of the client. The agency takes a huge part of it."

"I never knew such a thing existed, an agency for escorts?" Jan asks.

"Your new to this business, and that's what it is, a business Jan.

In a way, Mr. Junkett is, an agency, but he doesn't make money off us.

He wants his pals happy, he provides us to them, and in his own unique way gets a kick out of knowing what is going on behind closed doors."

"I would rather work with you, at Mr. Junkett's and not run all over meeting different men that sounds very risky in my opinion. Tell me more about Nick's friend Crissy."

"His name is Jim and he is a very nice guy, so far he has been paying me better than average, and he tries to keep me as happy as I do him."

"Monday, after classes, I am going to the unemployment office. I am going to give them my information; see if I can find some work and apply for it. Personally, I am not going to let myself get involved with something I do not feel comfortable with, like this agency stuff. I can't wait for Mary, she might never quit Crissy."

"She's wild Jan, taking risks, she told me about some of the risks she is willing to take."

"In my imagination, going out to meet a man who calls and describes the type of woman he wants some agency to send him sounds very risky. After all he could be a nut Crissy."

Let me see what mom is doing, I'll be right back."

Jan goes out of her room, she sees Judy asleep on the couch, papers in her hands. She returns to her room and picks up her phone.

"Mom is out; she wore herself out preparing for my party."

"I know you must be tired yourself Jan, we can talk more before school if you want to?"

"The more you tell me is for my own safety and consideration Crissy. You've become such a wonderful friend who I appreciate so much.

I don't know, the money, such a lot of money for your body. I'm really afraid of all the diseases out there that some guy could give you, me, or Mary."

"Yes there is disease, that's a fact, a lot of it can kill you, and we all know that Jan. Mr. Junkett insists the men show him and us their current test results from the health department."

"Wouldn't his test only be good for that moment, what about when he leaves and goes home? For all either of you know, he could be messing around with someone else, getting something that he could give you."

"True, something to think about, but for my situation with Jim, he told me that he prefers to be a one woman man. He wants only me, other than his wife who he describes as cold and distant. He says she is not seeing other men. I give, or try to give him what he wants so he will stay loyal to me."

"I don't know Jim, Crissy, but something about him, says don't trust him. If I say any more to Mary about bringing me money she would think I'm being jealous, and just trying to get her to quit so I could replace her."

"No one could talk to her now Jan, she has greed fever that blinds her to all risks, real or imagined."

"Don't say anything to her about our talk, no use to make her think we are trying to figure out a way to make her quit, or have Mr. Junkett fire her."

"Not a problem there, we meet tomorrow afternoon for another session at Mr. Junkett's. I won't even let on that I know she gave you the money, I'll leave that for her to bring up to me."

"Do you think she will say something to you Crissy?"

"Maybe, she likes to brag, and show off.

If she does tell me, I'll let her know my own way it was really tacky of her to give you money for your birthday."

I'll see you on Monday at class Jan, rest the weekend, you need it."

"I will get my resume finished so I can take it with me to the unemployment office."

"Good luck at the unemployment office, they have computers there, and you can search on them for jobs that you might be qualified for Jan."

"I'll find something, of course other jobs are not paying what you and Mary are making, I hope to find a job that I can do, it pays well, and hopefully I can save enough for college."

"Did you want me to keep you informed if an opening becomes available at Mr. Junkett's Jan?"

"Part of me wants to say yes, another part says not to get involved Crissy, I can't explain why I have bad feelings about becoming an escort. I don't condemn you, or Mary being one Crissy; I'm only telling you my own personal feelings."

Crissy laughs, "Part of you this, part of you that, I'll tell you one thing Jan, you see the money lying in your hand, you would forget those parts."

"If something might open up, tell me about it. If I've found a great job with possibilities of it leading to a great career, I more than likely will not pass it up Crissy."

"Not a bad decision Jan, there are times I do regret becoming an escort.

Always making up lies about what I do, my odd hours, it's stressful."

"I don't want to hide Crissy, doing that is stressful enough. My mom is keen when it comes to figuring me out, that mother's instinct she calls it, and the Doctor mentioned that too. Your mother hasn't figured out that you're up to something Crissy?"

"Mom isn't stupid, I know that Jan; I just avoid giving her any direct answers. If she asks me how work was, I tell her fine, it went well, and drop it. I hide my money until I have the chance to put it in my savings account. She does not open any of my mail. She has no idea how much I have in my checking, or savings."

"Doesn't it worry you that eventually your mom might find out what your doing Crissy?"

"Of course it does Jan, but right now I'm trying to not let anything affect me. I have to be at my best for Jim, that's what he pays me for."

"Sorry about all of the questions Crissy, how you feel doesn't mean I would feel that way. I don't judge you that wouldn't be right of me."

"I never thought you would judge me Jan, you are very different than me. If you never decide to be an escort, I wouldn't hold it against you."

"As much as I never hold it against you Crissy that you are an escort."

"Good night Jan, and again my love to you and happy birthday."

"Love to you too Crissy and thanks for the great presents, and most of all thanks for being a best friend."

Chapter 11

Two months later

Jan spends her weekend helping Judy with chores around the house and resting. Jan gets ready for another day of school. She takes the bus to school. When she gets off the bus, Crissy is waiting for her.

"Hi Jan, have a good weekend? Crissy hugs Jan.

"Sure did, Crissy, do you have anything new to share?"

Crissy and Jan walk to their class, "I found an escort agency that says they will be supportive to me, and I might try working for them."

Jan stops walking; she gives Crissy a shocked look, "I thought you were disgusted about how much an agency takes from you, and having to fleece the clients for more money?"

"I'm going to go talk to them after classes are over; I want to get more information. That's all I intend on doing at this point, is talk to them."

Crissy looks at her, "Come with me Jan, you could find out yourself what it's all about."

Jan stops walking she begins feeling tense. "I still believe the right thing for me to do is go to the unemployment office. I cannot get comfortable thinking about working for an agency right now Crissy. Besides, if Jim is paying you as much money you said he is, why are you even thinking about working for an agency? I do not get a good feeling about putting yourself in danger, or risking your health. I really think the love of money has gone to your head Crissy, your starting to act greedy."

Crissy smiles at Jan, she takes her hand, "Perhaps it's my own jealousy, wanting brag to Mary that I make more than she does, I do not really know Jan."

"To even think about bragging to her, is immature Crissy. I had more faith in you and your attitude about escort agencies that you have shared with me."

"I'll think about what you said Jan, you're my friend. I trust you, and you have given me all your trust. You also give me your advice, and I respect that. I hope you find a great job Jan you deserve it. You don't need more stress in your life being an escort."

They attend their classes not talking to one another. Their day ends, they walk together to the bus stop.

Crissy takes her hand, "I've thought about what you said Jan. I have decided your right. I love the money, which is a fact. I do not want to come across as greedy, and then get myself into trouble. It would be immature trying to impress Mary. She would find another way to brag about what she makes. It could develop into something that never ends."

Jan smiles at Crissy; she gives her hand a squeeze, "I'm proud of you Crissy, I thought you have more common sense than Mary.

I must get over to the unemployment office; I'll let you know what happens there when I'm done."

Jan quickly gives her a hug; she boards the bus sitting in front watching for her stop. When she gets off nearby the unemployment office, she sees a sign across the street in the window of Clark's Pharmacy. "Help wanted inquire within," she decides that she will ask about the job.

She stops at the cashier, "Can I help you find something?"

"Yes, I saw your help wanted sign, who may I speak to about it?"

"Go to our pharmacy in the back of the store. Ask for Mr. Clark, he's the one you will need to talk with about the job."

Jan stops for a moment making sure her dress is not a mess. She sees a small mirror in the cosmetic isle picking it up she checks her makeup.

Walking up to the pharmacy desk, she sees a man preparing prescriptions. She waits for his attention, he turns around seeing her, "Can I help you young lady?"

"Are you Mr. Clark, if so my name's Jan, I would like a moment to speak with you about your help wanted offer posted in your front window."

"I'm Mr. Clark, I would be happy to give you a quick interview Jan. Give me a moment to finish this prescription. Take a seat, and fill out our application."

She fills out the application; and places her resume with it.

Mr. Clark asks her to follow him to his office. "Sit down Jan while I look at your application."

She watches Mr. Clark look over her application.

He puts it down, "The job I'm offering is a pharmacy technician trainee. What do you think about training for that job?"

She looks at him, "I would enjoy helping your customers, help you with prescriptions. I know my job title is trainee, and I gladly accept that title. I will want to know what college subjects I need to take. Or any thing else you feel will help me learn more."

He writes on the back of her application. He stops writing "You are a senior in high school, could you work after school, and Saturdays Jan?"

"My parents gave me full permission to work; with the understanding, any job would not affect my schoolwork. Working after school, or Saturday's is not a problem Mr. Clark. I would have time to study, and complete assignments."

"I must say I'm very impressed with you Jan, I just posted the offer of work, so I need to give others an opportunity to apply. If I did hire you, starting pay would be ten dollars an hour, is that sufficient?"

Jan squirms in her chair, "That is more than sufficient Mr. Clark, I want to make enough to save and pay for at least two years of college after I graduate."

"I see, and that is a worthy goal Jan. what time after school, could you start working?"

"Some of my classes end at three, so I could be here by three thirty. I went to summer school getting extra credit, which lets me take fewer classes. I can work until you close Mr. Clark."

"We close at eight, you could work four and a half hours a day during the week. Saturdays you would work eight am until five pm."

"That gives me a thirty and a half hour week then Mr. Clark."

He smiles, "You're fast with math Jan that impresses me.

You would be working with me and my other registered pharmacist too. Both of us would make sure you know what we require you to learn. We have to regulate the hours you can work, and what you can do. One of us will supervise you, since you are a trainee. There are many things you can only do with under our supervision and not do alone."

Jan smiles at him, "I certainly wouldn't do anything without you or the other pharmacist right by my side Mr. Clark. I really need work, and I can't afford to make any mistakes, and I'm sure you wouldn't want me to make any either."

He finishes writing on her application, "Do you have any other questions Jan?"

Jan glances at her watch, "I've taken up a lot of your time Mr. Clark, I can't think of anything else, other than thank you for giving me consideration for the job. I assure you I will do my best to learn and be the employee you seek."

"I'll leave the sign in my window the rest of this week for others to apply Jan. If I decide to hire you, I will call you Friday evening, and if I hired you, could you start working Saturday morning?"

Jan smiles, "Yes Mr. Clark, I'll talk to my mother she is very supportive, and let her know. If you hire me for the job, I will be here at eight am on Saturday."

"You will need to bring your social security card and any identification that has your photo on it. We need those to verify you're a citizen, that's the law, do you have those documents?"

"I do Mr. Clark; I'll have them in my purse so you can copy them."

"Thank you for stopping in Jan, I'll let you know either way on this position."

She stands up, and offers her hand, and Mr. Clark shakes it. She smiles at him and walks to the exit. Pausing a moment, she looks back at Mr. Clark, "Thank you again sir for your consideration."

Jan walks outside; she stares at the help wanted sign. She has a hopeful wish that he will hire her. Her reality is that she is still in high school, and lacks any job experience.

She walks down to the unemployment office when she goes in; she writes her name on a sign in form and sits down.

The clerk calls her, she returns to the desk, "I want to post a resume. This is my first time here, is there anything you can suggest which will help me?"

The clerk points towards the computers "Create a sign in name, and a personal identification code. You use both to access your information each time you come here and search for a job."

Jan smiles, she sits in front of the computer, creating her sign on name, and personal code. She carefully fills in her experience and education.

When finished, she creates words for a hit list that might match her to a posted job. Nothing posted matches her hit list words.

She thinks to herself "I'm not having any luck here finding a job. Many of the jobs posted require me to have already graduated. To be considered for an interview some employers want experience I don't have."

Jan signs off the computer, thanks the clerk, leaving to ride the bus back home.

Jan gets home; Judy is busy in the kitchen. "I saw a job offered for a pharmacy technician trainee at Clark's Pharmacy, so I applied, and was interviewed. I also went to the unemployment office, and registered with them."

"That would be a great job Jan, how did your interview go?"

"I lack a lot of experience but I told him I'm willing to learn if he hires me. He said I could work after school and on Saturdays."

"Forty hours Jan?"

"No, just thirty and a half mom, he will pay me ten dollars an hour."

"Twelve hundred gross, less taxes, at least a thousand a month Jan, not bad for a high school girl."

Jan sighs, she sits watching her in the kitchen, "Not what Crissy or Mary is making, but I can't wait for Mary to quit, whenever that might be."

Judy smiles, she gives her a hug, "Maybe you wouldn't really enjoy the type of work they do Jan. Please do not take the trainee job, and then quit to work with Crissy and not feel good about it. I hear a lot of apprehension in your voice."

She rubs her hands anxiously, "I've talked with Crissy more about it. I do not feel comfortable about it or comfortable about Mary working there. I feel I have made the right decision. I might not get this trainee job, at least I tried, and I will not give up. I am going to call Crissy so I can tell her about it.

Call me when dinner's ready."

Judy smiles at Jan, "It won't be long until dinner's ready, and take your time."

Jan calls Crissy, she answers, "Hi Jan, did you find anything at the unemployment office?"

"No, most jobs if not all of them want someone who has finished high school. However I saw a job offer posted at Clark's Pharmacy, so I applied for it."

"Working as a clerk Jan?"

"Something a lot better than just a clerk Crissy, a pharmacy technician trainee, and he will pay me ten dollars an hour for that job."

"Your moving up in this world Jan, do you think you have a chance to get it?"

"He is leaving the sign up until Friday. He will let me know either way after he interviews anyone else who applies. I am not going to let myself get over excited or stressed out if I don't get it. I know I have fewer qualifications than others do who apply. At least I had an interview, and I hope I impressed Mr. Clark that I'm willing to learn."

"Good luck Jan, I hope it will work out for you, let me know."

"Thanks Crissy, I hope it works out too, but if it doesn't, we graduate soon, I might have to wait until after that to look for something. I could take several courses a semester at our community college and work too."

"Did you ask your dad to help you out; maybe he would pay for some of your courses?"

"I gave a big hint when I asked him if I could apply for work at Mr. Junkett's Crissy. I also hinted that I needed to make money for college, and I would be helping mom out too.

He hasn't said a thing to me since then, except tell him if I find a job."

She hears a knock on her door, "Dinner's ready Jan, so come and eat now."

"I've got to go eat dinner Crissy, I'll let you know what happens, and I'll see you Thursday."

Jan and Judy do not talk during their dinner.

"Would you like to have a second serving Jan?"

"I'm pretty full mom; you gave me a lot of food. I'll help you wash the dishes and put them away."

"Jan, you never said anything about finding any work you could apply for at the unemployment office."

"I posted my resume, with what experience I have, did a job search, but nothing came up."

Judy looks at her while wiping the dishes dry, "I know you're hoping Mr. Clark will call you Jan.

Do not put all your hope on his job. You don't need to become depressed if you don't get it."

"Of course I hope for that job mom, my lack of experience makes it hard for me to find any job. I'll keep stopping at the unemployment office every day after school anyhow"

"At least you have a plan Jan. You can look in the paper too. Have you considered applying for work at one of the burger places in town?"

"They don't pay anything mom, just minimum wages. I really need more than that to save for college."

"Something of anything is better than nothing Jan, keep positive. I'll ask my friends at work if they might know if someone is looking for help."

"Crissy asked me if I spoke to dad about paying for my school. I told her I gave him a hint that I needed the job to pay for college, but he hasn't said anything to me."

"If he calls Jan, I will drop my own hint for you. He is very good at his guilt trips; it is about time I get better at my own about him paying for your college. It might take you more than four years, and if you get good grades you could qualify for a scholarship, and then transfer?"

"If you tell him community college, it isn't as expensive. I am beating my brains out now to maintain a B+ average, In order to qualify for a scholarship I need A+. I will work harder to bring up my grade average, and try to qualify for a scholarship."

"You can also ask one of your teachers if they know about any grants you could apply for. A grant will pay your school in full; and you wouldn't have to pay it back, like you would if it was a student loan."

"No one in my senior class has mentioned a grant, but they might not know about them either. I'll ask the principal if he has any information about them that he can give me."

"I'm sure he does Jan, that is their job, besides making sure you graduate. They want you to go to college; it's the only way to succeed."

"If, and that is a big if I get hired and can train as a pharmacy technician, then Mr. Clark might know about a grant too."

"You can always ask him, even if he doesn't hire you Jan, that is if your serious about making pharmacy your career."

"Ten dollars an hour to start, just as a trainee, I can only imagine what I would be paid being a technician, or pharmacist."

"Registered pharmacist pays you a lot more Jan, if you want to go to the top, why should you settle for the middle?"

"I have to start somewhere mom, right now I have to start at the bottom. I intend on making it to the top, no matter how long it takes. I'm going to bed now, so good night and I love you."

"Love you too Jan, you're a wonderful young woman and daughter I'm so very proud of you."

Jan blows a kiss to Judy, "Thanks mom, it was a great dinner as usual."

Chapter 12

Jan spends her week at school, studying, nervous that it's Friday.

"Today's the big day Jan, I hope that Mr. Clark calls you early."

"He opens at eight, so perhaps soon mom."

The phone ringing startles Jan and Judy.

Jan says, "I'll answer mom, it could be Mr. Clark."

"Good morning Jan, its Crissy, I just wanted to call to wish you luck."

Jan breathes a sigh of relief, "You scared me Crissy, I was startled by the phone ringing, and I didn't look at my caller ID. I was hoping it was Mr. Clark calling."

"You told me he would call, I won't tie up your line Jan, anyhow, best of luck to you."

"I appreciate your thoughts Crissy, No matter what, I'll call you and let you know what happens."

"It was really nice of her to call and wish you luck Jan. Too bad you couldn't work with her, she's became such a good friend who's there for you."

Jan sits on the couch, "The more I think about it, I'm glad I didn't get the job mom, Crissy says it's very stressful. Even though she doesn't show it, I feel it from her."

Judy smiles at Jan as she finishes the dishes, "You have enough stress, now that you're getting close to finishing your senior year. I hope any job you do work at won't be too much for you."

Judy picks up her briefcase, she walks to the door, "I'll be working at my office Jan, call me later."

"I've got to get busy; washing my laundry will take my mind off of Mr. Clark calling."

Jan watches television while she washes her laundry. She gets more and more nervous as the day proceeds she carefully folds her laundry putting it away. Glancing at her watch Jan thinks to herself, "Almost four; I wonder why Mr. Clark hasn't called?"

She decides to take a shower, wash her hair. She just steps into the shower, when the phone rings, her heart races. Caller ID shows Mr. Clark is calling. Wrapping a towel around herself, she quickly picks up the phone.

"Good afternoon Mr. Clark, I hope you're having a good day."

"Hello Jan, I wanted you to know I've finished all interviews, and made my decision who I want to hire. I have decided to hire you Jan, I feel that you are very mature, more than willing to learn, and want to learn. I believe that if I give you a chance, you would be a fine pharmacist someday."

She sits on her bed, the phone in her hand, her head spinning.

She composes herself, "Mr. Clark, I truly appreciate your trust, I will do everything I can to quickly learn to do what you ask. I cannot thank you enough for choosing me. I am sure there were others who were more than qualified."

"Jan, be at the pharmacy, Saturday at seven thirty. Ms. Lake, our other pharmacist will copy your documents and finish your paperwork. You'll be ready by eight when we open."

"May I wear the same dress Mr. Clark, or would you prefer I wear something else?"

"You can wear that dress Jan. If you feel more comfortable, a simple and modest blouse, and pants are fine."

"Thank you so very much for your trust; I'll do my utmost best to show you that your decision to hire me was the right one."

"I'll see you tomorrow Jan, you'll do just fine."

Her heart is racing she dials Crissy, "Hi Jan has Mr. Clark called you yet?"

"Yes, Crissy, he hired me, I start working tomorrow. I'm so excited I can hardly talk."

"Wonderful Jan, I know you'll do the best you can. I am so glad things have worked out for you. Doing that work is much better for you Jan, not what Mary and I do."

"I'm a little jealous about the money you two make Crissy. Until there might be an opening at Mr. Junkett's I'll take this job."

"Jan, please, listen to me, I don't want you to give up an opportunity for a great career to be an escort. You have said yourself; you didn't feel it was your thing."

Jan takes in a breath, "Crissy, I was releasing some of my own frustration, forgive me."

"If you had gotten the job, you would know what frustration is Jan."

"If it's that bad, why do you keep on doing it?"

"Give me a call Sunday and let me know how your first day goes Jan."

"I will Crissy, and I'm so anxious for mom to come home so I can tell her."

I will let you go then Jan, and best of luck in your new job at Mr. Clark's drugstore. "

Jan finishes dusting and cleaning wondering why Crissy expresses so much frustration about being an escort, but keeps doing it. "Must be money, money, and more money," Jan thinks to herself.

Judy opens the door, "I'm so glad your home mom," Jan gives Judy a hug.

"Well, what a welcome, you must have good news then, right Jan?"

"Mr. Clark hired me; I start at seven thirty in the morning. I have to show them my identification that proves it's legal for me to work."

"Everything has to be legal Jan. I'm glad you understand that."

"I'm going to get to bed early tonight; I want to be ready for tomorrow."

"Did you decide what to wear Jan?"

"I asked him if he wanted me to wear the same dress I wore to my interview. He said that was fine or I can wear pants with a modest blouse."

Judy looks at her, "Pants will be comfortable this time Jan. Wear your new dress another time, or when he suggests it."

"I'll look through my pants and chose nice pair that look good with a white blouse."

"That will look very professional Jan. Look at others who work for Mr. Clark, see what they are wearing. His business would not be appropriate for flashy clothes."

"I would not dare dress flashy mom, that's for sure. I'm going to bed mom, good night, and thanks so much for your support."

"Good night Jan, I'll be home tomorrow taking care of my own chores. I'll look forward to hear about your first day at your new job when you get home."

Jan puts on her nightgown, lying on her bed she looks around her room, so dark with the lights out. She sets her clock.

The alarm startles her; she wipes her eyes in disbelief that six am came so fast.

Judy is cleaning in the kitchen, "Your up early mom, did you have a problem sleeping?"

"No Jan, I wanted to see how you looked. Your choice of those pants and blouse is perfect. You're looking like a pharmacist." She says with a laugh in her voice.

"I have a long way to go for that mom; I'll see how I like this job. If I do, I'll take college courses to be a pharmacist."

Jan opens her purse to be sure she has her social security card, photo identification card from school. She thinks to herself "I really do hope I like this job, and will do well."

Judy gives her a hug, "Eat before you go Jan, and take enough money to buy yourself lunch."

Jan finishes her breakfast; she looks at her watch, and its six forty five.

She quickly picks up her purse, "I'll see you later mom, and I don't want to be late, love you."

She keeps hoping traffic will not make her late.

She gets off the bus near the pharmacy; she nervously looks at her watch, seven forty five. Rushing to the door, she looks inside, and all but a few lights are off. Knocking on the door, she tries to see if anyone is inside.

She hears a voice behind her, "You must be Jan, our new trainee?"

She turns around; a well-dressed woman is approaching her. "You must be Ms, Lake, I'm happy to meet you."

"Call me Trish, Jan, and come inside with me. You can get your paperwork finished so when Mr. Clark gets here everything is finished. You look very nice today Jan."

"I asked mom to check me out before I left today, I wanted to look professional for my first day Trish."

"Mr. Clark will be pleased Jan that you have that attitude."

Trish unlocks the door; she quickly walks to the back and disables the alarm system. Jan waits for her near the front door.

Trish calls her, "Turn the lock on the front door Jan, make sure it's locked.

Come back here to my office, your paperwork is ready for you to fill out."

Jan locks the door; she walks to a lighted room. Trish is sitting at a desk placing papers on top of it.

Jan gives her social security card, school photo identification to Trish.

"Take the papers in front of you and fill them out Jan. If you do not understand anything, let me know.

I will be happy to help you. While your doing that, I'll copy your cards."

Jan fills out each paper in front of her.

She hands them to Trish. "These are pretty well self explanatory. You can double check them, I believe I've filled in everything right."

Trish hands Jan her cards, "You didn't miss a thing Jan, not bad since you never had a previous job."

Jan smiles, "I've watched my mom with her filling out her employment forms Trish."

She pulls out a file cabinet drawer putting an envelope inside of it with her name on it, "In here is where we put your employee file, and papers you filled out. Everything is confidential, only Mr. Clark or I have access to it. He marks paydays on our calendar, so you know when you are going to get your pay. We can direct deposit money to your checking, or savings account if you want us to. After your three-month probation period is finished, you are eligible for our medical, and life insurance program. Mr. Clark pays most of it you pay a small portion. Either of us will make sure you get forms to fill out to apply for the insurance."

Trish excuses herself, she walks towards the front door, "Mr. Clark's here Jan, he will tell you who your going to work with first, either myself, or him."

Jan and Trish walk to the front; he turns around, "Welcome Jan, I'm glad you've met Trish Lake, my other pharmacist. You can call me Bruce or her Trish in private. Mr. Clark, Ms. Lake in front of our customers."

Jan smiles, she extends her hand, "Thank you Bruce for a warm welcome. Trish has been very helpful to me. She explained everything to me this morning."

"If you have any questions about anything Jan, ask me, or Trish."

"I will Bruce, do you prefer I work with Trish, or you this morning?"

He pauses a moment, "Work with Trish this morning Jan. After lunch, until we close, I will work with you."

Trish turns to her, "Let's go to the pharmacy Jan. I will show you the basics on our cash register, how to operate it. We like you to greet our clients a certain way, so I will show you what we prefer. You will take their prescriptions, and give them to us."

She shows Jan how they want her to take the prescription, and give it to either her, or Bruce. She shows her how to input the prescription code into the cash register. A customer walks up, Jan watches while Trish asks how she can help, and they give her a prescription. Trish tells them to please sit down and wait for her to tell them it's ready. She takes the prescription to Bruce.

Jan looks at her, "May I assist the next customer please? Tell me if I need to improve doing anything Trish."

Customers walk up and Jan assists them.

She looks at Trish, "You greeted our customers with a smile, you're a natural Jan, I haven't see anything yet that you need to improve. If you need help, I will be close enough so you can call me."

Trish goes to the back to help Bruce fill prescriptions. Jan keeps busy helping customers at the desk. She watches them look in her direction talking to one another.

After filling an order she hands it to Jan, "When you finish this order Jan, take an hour for lunch."

She finds it hard to believe it is lunchtime already. "Being busy makes the time pass so fast" is her thought.

After finishing, she walks outside looking for a place to eat. She sees Murphy's Burgers at the end of the block. While walking, she calls Crissy, "Hi Jan how's your first day at work?"

"So far, everything's going well, at least I haven't made any major mistakes."

"Did you prepare any prescriptions Jan?"

"No silly, I can't do that; "I take the prescription, give it to whoever is available. I take the customer's money or credit card and get them on their way. If I have time I try to watch Mr. Clark, or Ms. Lake prepare the prescription."

"They are the pharmacists there who supervise you?"

"Mr. Clark owns the pharmacy, and Ms. Lake is his other pharmacist."

Your not bored yet Jan?"

"Did you expect me to be bored Crissy? I have been too busy to be bored."

Jan hears a voice talking in the background of Crissy's phone.

"It sounds like your busy Crissy, I'm sorry for interrupting. I have to eat lunch, I'll call you later."

Jan realizes Crissy hung up on her without saying good-bye.

Jan wonders to herself "What was going on with Crissy? The voice in the background sounded like a man trying to talk to her."

She eats and returns to finish out her day. Trish is waiting at the front of the store for her.

"This afternoon work in the back with Bruce, we will reverse our roles. I will be giving you the customer's prescription, and then you hand it to him and watch how he prepares it."

She smiles at Trish, "I will do exactly what I'm told to do, not a problem." Jan works the rest of her afternoon watching Bruce count pills, measuring liquids.

He carefully explains to her what he is doing, "It's almost five Jan, and you have done very well for your first day. We look forward to seeing you after school on Monday."

"My day sure went fast Bruce; I was too busy to be bored. I learned a lot from both of you. Thank you, I appreciate your patience."

Bruce smiles at her, "You learn fast, which is why I hired you Jan. If you decide to make pharmacology your career, I can see you being your own boss one day, owning your own business."

"I appreciate your confidence in me for that Bruce. I will need to go to school eventually, but in the meantime, I am a willing student here to learn more. I'll see you Monday after school."

"Good bye for now Jan and job well done." Bruce says.

She has to wait for ten minutes for her bus to arrive. She calls Crissy, "Your calling again Jan, any problems?"

She looks down the street for the bus, "Everything went good today Crissy. Did you realize you hung up earlier on me and did not even say good-bye to me? I thought I heard a man talking in the background, were you working?"

"I was sort of busy Jan, sorry about that, I'll try to explain later."

"I wish you would explain now Crissy. I hope you don't think I'm insisting that you tell me about your personal business?"

"Too personal is right Jan, like I said, I'll try to explain to you later."

"Are you working with that escort agency Crissy?"

"My schedule is really hectic Jan, let me call you."

Jan restrains her curiosity, and anger at Crissy. She thinks to herself "I wonder if she was with a man from that escort agency? I hope if that is the case, she is being careful, I would hate for her to get hurt."

The bus arrives; she gets on and starts her ride home.

Chapter 13

Jan arrives home, Judy's in the kitchen, "Hi mom, everything went great at work, and it seems I made a good impression."

Judy turns to look at her, "I knew you would Jan, I'm happy everything went well."

Jan sits at the dinner table, watching her prepare dinner.

Judy sits a plate in front of her, "You act like something is bothering you Jan, would you care to tell me about it?"

Jan looks at her food, she looks at Judy, "I'm worried about Crissy, I called her and she wasn't acting like herself. She was very short with me, as if I was bothering her. She hung up on me and didn't even say good bye."

Judy rubs her shoulder, "We all have our good days and our bad days Jan. She might have been having a bad day and didn't feel like talking about it when you called."

Judy sits down next to her "It's better for you, if you concentrate on your job Jan. It is obvious to me that you and Crissy are taking different directions in life. Her work is not the same as yours Jan. You said she was under a lot of stress. You never have told me exactly what she's doing and It's apparent to me something about her job bothers you."

Jan stares across the living room and barely eating. She looks at Judy, "I'm glad I don't work with Crissy, despite our friendship bond this year mom. I keep being worried she's getting deeper than she should, and I can't do anything to stop it."

"Have you tried talking to her?"

"Several times, but she evades my questions, or pretty much tells me it isn't my business."

Judy finishes dinner, taking her plate to the sink "When your ready Jan, you can talk to me, I won't judge either of you girls. I am your mother, and a mother's instinct inside me says that something's wrong. I want you to know I'm here for both of you, if you need me."

Three months later

Jan is very independent at work; she helps Bruce and Trish prepare prescriptions with their guidance and observation.

One day, when she leaves work Crissy is waiting for her. "Crissy, you don't look well, I've noticed the past three past months you've lost a lot of weight. I wanted to talk to you about it, but I thought you were on one of your diets, and it wasn't my business."

Crissy takes her hand, "We need to talk Jan, let's walk for a while. "I have not been truthful to you. I needed to talk to someone. You are my best friend; I know I can talk to you in total confidence. Remember I told you, I was thinking about working with Mary?"

"Yes, working with her for an agency. You asked me to think about working for them, if I was still interested in being an escort. I told you then that I had a bad feeling about it. Besides, I thought the way you talked that you were not going to work with an agency Crissy?"

"I know Jan, greed got to me. I have been really stupid and greedy for money, this year, and last year. I have been having sex several times a week with a man I met through the agency. I have been making fifteen hundred a week meeting Jim, and the other guy Jan."

"When did you first meet him Crissy?"

"Last year, we met several times through the agency. He offered to double what I earned if he did not have to go through them to meet me. He also offered me triple pay if he did not have to wear a condom. I accepted his offers, and quit working for them.

I told Jim the birth control pills were making me sick. I insisted he had to wear a condom. He did not like it, but he reluctantly agreed. Recently I have started feeling a lot worse. I asked the other person I met to show me a recent health report. He keeps telling me his doctor is busy, or he hasn't had the time to get a follow up health report."

"Crissy, you should go to the free clinic yourself and let them tell you if anything is affecting your weight."

"That's why I came here today Jan. I want you to go with me to the clinic. Will you do that for me?"

"I'll call mom and tell her I won't be home right away."

Crissy takes her arm, "Don't tell her where we're going Jan, It's been hard not feeling well, and trying to hide it from my mother. She noticed my weight loss and has been giving me lectures about not eating."

"The free clinic stays open twenty four hours Crissy; let's go there now, please."

"Ok, Jan, tell your mother, we're going to talk a while, and you'll be home after we finish."

Jan calls her mother, "Crissy stopped by after work. We're going to talk for a while, and then I'll come home, is that alright?"

"Of course Jan, be sure to be home by no later than eight."

"Mom said it's alright for me to stay with you Crissy. She wants me to be home by eight."

They walk into the clinic; the receptionist looks up, "How can I help you ladies?"

Crissy leans over the reception desk, "I need to see a Doctor as soon as possible."

The receptionist gives her a clipboard "Fill out the papers on this, when your finished bring them to me please. You can be seated over there," she points to a private room with a desk in it.

They walk to the room "Wait outside Jan; I'll fill out my papers. When I am finished, we will sit together."

Twenty minutes later, Crissy comes out, she takes the clipboard to the receptionist sitting it on her desk, the receptionist tells her, "Be seated, the nurse will be with you shortly."

Crissy is very nervous she sits with Jan,

"Hopefully the Doctor will see you soon Crissy. I thought you were covered by your mother's work insurance?"

"I am covered by her insurance Jan. The last thing I need is mom finding what kind of work I've been doing."

"Your mom isn't stupid Crissy, she has noticed you have lost weight, and asked you about it. Haven't you realized she suspects something's wrong with you?"

"Mom has been busy at her work, and other things, she noticed, I told her that I wasn't eating as much. She asked me if I would start eating more, I told her yes, she was satisfied with my answer."

The nurse calls Crissy's name she walks towards her, looking back at Jan smiling.

Ten minutes later Crissy returns, "She weighed me, took my temperature. The nurse took a blood sample. She sent it to the lab; I have to wait for the Doctor to get the lab report, before he will talk to me."

"I hope it doesn't take too long to get the lab results, we have been here more than an hour now. I 'm not sure mom will let me stay too much after eight Crissy."

"If you have to go home, and then go, I'll be alright Jan. Please try to stay as long as you can, I need your support."

"I'll stay as long as I can Crissy."

Another twenty minutes pass, the nurse calls Crissy. She tells her the Doctor will see her now.

Crissy nervously walks to the desk, "Can my best friend go with me?"

The receptionist looks at Crissy; and Jan "Sorry, we're only allowed to let direct family go with you Crissy."

"Sorry, I'm so nervous; I meant to say she's my sister, who's my best friend."

"Alright, your sister can go with you."

Crissy motions to Jan, she takes her arm. They follow the nurse to a room where they sit down, holding hands while they wait.

A few moments pass, the Doctor and nurse come into the room; they sit across from them. He has the papers Crissy filled out, "This is your sister, is that correct Crissy?"

"Correct Doctor, and my best friend. I want her to be here with me. Did you get my lab test results?"

The Doctor looks at the papers, "First I need to ask you Crissy are you currently having a sexual relationship with a man?"

"Yes, Doctor, I am."

The Doctor sits back "I have another question, are you having safe sex with him?"

Crissy lowers her head "No Doctor, he hasn't been wearing a condom."

The Doctor writes notes on his papers, "How well do you know this man Crissy?"

"I met him last year Doctor."

"Have you had unprotected sex with any other men Crissy?"

"I've had unprotected sex with two others, Doctor, but some time ago I told one he had to start wearing a condom."

He sits back in his chair "Would you tell me why you let two men have unprotected sex with you and then unprotected with a third man who you now insist has to wear a condom?"

She looks up at him, "I prefer to not tell you, it is personal information."

He pauses a minute "My next question might offend you Crissy. Are you a prostitute?"

She glares at him, and angrily blurts out, "Escort Doctor, I'm an escort, not a hooker or prostitute!"

"Have you worked for an escort agency, or are you independent?"

"I had unprotected sex with two business friends of an individual in town who runs a private escort service. I worked for an agency and I quit after I started meeting a man I met through them privately and saw only those three men Doctor, no one else."

The Doctor pauses after writing notes, "Crissy, the blood tests show that you have two sexually transmitted infections, both of them are affecting your health. You've been sick for a while Crissy, I would say in my opinion you were infected some time ago."

Crissy fear in her face looks at him and says, "Infections, what infections Doctor. All of the men I've been seeing are clean."

"How long ago did you ask them for their tests that showed they were clean?"

Crissy looks down, "When I first started having sex with them Doctor."

"You haven't insisted they show you anything since you first met either of them?

Crissy tightly holds Jan's hand, "No Doctor, now please, tell me what infections I have."

He excuses himself and leaves the room. In a few minutes, he brings with him another paper. He lies it down on the counter, "I asked the lab to double check your blood tests. Both times the results were the same. "I hate to give you bad news all at once Crissy, but your life is at risk here. The tests show you are infected with acquired immune disorder syndrome or AIDS, and hepatitis C."

She begins to sob uncontrollably while Jan sits and holds her.

After a twenty-minute interlude, she looks at the Doctor, "You just gave me a death sentence Doctor, plain and simple."

"There are drugs on the market and available Crissy. They help, but do not cure, and my main concern is in some cases hepatitis C can develop into cirrhosis of the liver, which can be fatal. The type of AIDS you have is a rare strain and symptoms caused by the virus can develop fairly fast, like they have in your case."

She looks at the Doctor, tears streaming down her face, "Is it possible that the tests are wrong? I keep hoping I'll wake up from a horrible nightmare, and none of this happened."

"I asked our lab to run the tests twice Crissy I had to make very sure before I said anything to you."

Jan holds on to Crissy trying to console her as she sobs.

She sits up, looks at the Doctor, "I would have never dreamed this would happen, I gave a lot of trust Doctor. Obviously I was beyond stupid trusting as much as I did."

"Another thing Crissy, one of the three men might have infected you. The health department will have to contact all of them so they can be tested, and treated if they are infected. We need the name and address of the man you work for locally. The law might investigate what he's been doing."

"Oh, my, what a mess, I don't want to tell, but I understand that I have to. I hope there aren't any others who were infected."

"We won't know until we have names, address, phone numbers, any personal information Crissy."

Crissy has her head on Jan's chest; she is running her hands through her hair.

"Am I at risk by touching her Doctor?"

"Only if you come into contact with her body fluids, like saliva, or blood, then you would risk infection."

"Should I take a blood test too Doctor?" Jan asks.

"See the nurse at the front desk I will tell her to arrange it right now Jan, while I finish talking with Crissy."

Jan leaves the room.

The Doctor sits watching Crissy sob and cry, he hands her tissues waiting until she composes herself.

Crissy finally looks at him, "I don't know what I'll tell my mother. I did not want her to know I am an escort. I don't want her to think I'm a whore, or a slut."

"She's your mother, and most mothers understand under the worst of circumstances Crissy. If you want to bring her in with you, then we all can discuss this in private. You have options for medications that are right for you.

You must immediately stop working as an escort, or having sex with anyone, even if they use a condom."

"I'll die eventually, that's life, but I don't want to die at eighteen Doctor."

"Of course not, AIDS affects your immune system; the drugs we give you to take will help. Many people who have AIDS continue to live productive lives Crissy. Proper diet and medication helps a lot of people with hepatitis live normal lives."

"Somewhat normal lives, isn't that what you mean Doctor? I personally don't think anyone with AIDS, or hepatitis C lives normally after they find out their affected by either virus."

"Everyone has a different description of normal Crissy. Many years ago, AIDS was a certain death sentence, so was hepatitis. New drugs help anyone affected by them to live the best they can. It might not be considered normal by some, but to those affected, they are able to work, be a productive person."

"Here's a paper to write down names, and all information about any men you've had sexual contact with. The health department investigation will not tell them where the information came from, or who gave it to them. You can be assured to remain anonymous."

Crissy manages a smile, "Yea, right Doctor, I'm one of two girls having sex at the local man's place. If I just disappear, then they will figure it out. I could care less about the agency finding out."

"I'll need the other girls name too Crissy, she might be at risk. If you're her friend, giving us her name might save her."

"Could I just tell her myself Doctor, and not have her contacted by the health department and get too upset?"

"Write her name down Crissy, with the other names. Let us do our job; if you want to alert her before we do, we insist you do it as soon as possible."

Crissy fills out the form with the names and addresses; she gives it to the Doctor.

"Here are your prescriptions Crissy, you must start these medications immediately. The pharmacy will give you pamphlets to read about any complications."

Crissy thanks him, and walks out of his office. Jan is waiting for her.

"I'm sure glad you were here Jan, I have to start taking all these medicines."

"First thing you need to do Crissy is to get the prescriptions filled. The pharmacy is right next door, we won't have to run all over town."

Jan waits outside while she gives her prescriptions to the receptionist. '

"I have to tell Mary, she's the one who encouraged me, and told me about that damn agency."

"Did the pharmacy say how long until they have your prescriptions ready Crissy?"

"They said within the half hour Jan, so is it possible you could wait a bit longer?"

Jan appearing nervous looks at her watch, "I'll call mom, and tell her just one hour more Crissy."

She calls Judy, "Just be careful and tell Crissy I said hello."

Jan tries to console Crissy, "Did your blood test come back alright Jan?"

"Yes, Crissy, it did, I'm alright. I understand now how I can get infected; I just have to be careful."

A man comes to the pharmacy door, "Crissy your prescriptions are ready for you to pick up now."

She picks up her prescriptions and instructions.

"I hate to leave you Crissy, but I should go home now."

"I understand Jan, and I really appreciate your being here for me, keep this secret for now, I'll decide when to talk to Mary, and of course my mother too."

Jan gives her a hug, "Let me know if I can help you in any way Crissy."

"Not much you can do for me Jan, I'm doomed. I appreciate that you went with me to the clinic. If you hadn't been with me, I would have thrown myself under a bus by now."

"Do not say that Crissy! I hope you're not serious?"

"More like damn depressed Jan, I have to vent somehow."

"Getting told what you did Crissy, being angry and depressed, and venting is normal. Just do not say you are going to commit suicide. It hurts me to see you this way. There's nothing I can do for you, other than listen."

"I'm sorry Jan; I'm not venting my anger on you intentionally."

"I appreciate you listening to me Jan. You correct me when I am wrong, and praise me when I am right. Thank you."

"Your welcome Crissy, it's the least I can do."

Chapter 14

Crissy drives home; her thoughts are "I just don't know what to say to mom, or how to say anything. She will be so disappointed in me."

She arrives home, and does not see her mother's car, "Maybe mom's working overtime, and hasn't had the time to call me."

She decides to call Mary, "Crissy, it's been a long time since we've talked, I've wondered about you, and how you have been?"

"I need to talk to you, preferably in private. Is it possible we can get together tonight?"

After a long pause, "I have one more client to meet. How about I call you when I am finished, we can meet then."

"Go ahead and call, mom isn't home yet. She's probably working overtime."

Still sitting in her car, she hangs up her phone just as her mother pulls into the driveway.

"Crissy, what are you doing out here? I was so worried about you I drove around looking for you."

"I had sort of an emergency mom, let's go inside and talk." She and her mother get out of their cars and go into their house.

Laura looks at her, "What kind of emergency did you have Crissy?"

She walks over to the couch, Laura follows her, "Mom, sit down, and I'll tell you."

"You must be very hungry, or did you eat somewhere else Crissy?"

She takes a napkin out of her purse, "Mom, you have been asking me about my weight loss. You have lectured me about not eating."

She wipes tears from her eyes, "I've been feeling sick for a while mom. I asked Jan to go with me to the free clinic on the other side of town."

Laura's body language shows she is uncomfortable. She shifts her position on the couch, "Why would you go to the free clinic Crissy? My insurance covers you; I just do not understand what has been going on with you. I have suspected you are not eating. I thought you were becoming bulimic or anorexic."

"How I wish I could confess that to you mom, but it's far more serious."

"Crissy, we've always had an open dialogue where I've told you since childhood that nothing and I do mean nothing had to be a secret between us. I feel like your keeping secrets from me, is that true?"

Crissy lowers her head, she does not look at her, "When I was at the clinic, the Doctor ordered blood tests to help him find out why I haven't been feeling good. The lab double-checked my blood tests mom. It wasn't good news about my health."

Her phone rings, it startles her; she sees Mary's number on her caller ID, "My client cancelled, I'm free now Crissy, where do you want to meet?"

"Call me back in a few moments Mary."

"Mom, I will finish telling you what happened. I have to talk to Mary first. I will not be that long, go ahead and start dinner. I'll be back by the time dinner's ready."

Laura looks at her in disbelief, "Crissy, why is she so important at this moment, I'm very worried about you. You start telling me the Doctor gave you bad news about your health, now you want to stop and run off and talk to Mary. I'm your mother, I need know before she does."

"I'm not going to tell her anything about going to the clinic, or my health mom. I have something else very important I need to tell her in person, not over the phone. Please don't be mad at me."

She looks at Laura while she walks to the door, "I'll talk with Mary really fast mom.

I promise to finish telling you what the Doctor said."

She rushes out of the house before Laura can say anything more.

Her phone rings when she starts getting into her car, "Where are you, where do you want to meet me Crissy?"

She starts her car and restrains her anger at Mary's attitude, "I'm leaving home right now, meet me in the parking lot behind Murphy's Grocery store, Mary."

"I should be there in about ten minutes Crissy."

She sees Mary's car in the parking lot, she drives up next to her. She opens her passenger door.

Mary gets in sitting next to her.

"Mary, I wanted to talk to you myself, rather than you find out from someone else."

"Talk to me about what yourself Crissy, I really don't like drama Crissy and I wish you wouldn't play your drama game with me. I hope it's important we met so fast."

"Mary, please, I'm not trying to be dramatic."

"What did you mean when you said find out from someone else? What are you referring to Crissy, is someone saying things or spreading rumors about me being an escort?"

"After I tell you, decide for yourself if it is drama. Mary, I have not been feeling well since early this year. I have tried keeping it a secret, not telling anyone. I went to the free clinic and they told me that I have AIDS, and hepatitis C. Karl, the agency client, I have been with since last year could have infected me. He showed me his tests when we first met and they said he was clean, I felt secure, and safe. I decided to tell Jim I had to stop taking birth control pills because they were making me sick, and he would have to wear a condom."

"I know Jim didn't like that Crissy."

"No, he did not Mary; he started wearing a condom anyhow. I'm damn glad he did. I had unsafe sex with Nick too Mary, it could have been any of them"

"Are you afraid I could be infected by Nick, Crissy?"

"That's part of the reason Mary; I had to give your name, Nick Karl, and Jim's names. Any of you might have a communicable disease. It's better to be safe, than sorry. The health department sends a letter to everyone to be tested. All of you will be told you could have been exposed to a communicable disease."

Mary's tears fall, she looks at Crissy, "I feel so responsible for this Crissy. I asked you to be an escort. I also encouraged you to work for the agency. Will you ever forgive me for that?"

Crissy takes her hand, "Your not responsible Mary, please don't feel that way. It was my decision to work for the agency. It was my decision allowing all of them to have sex with me, without a condom. I wanted to tell you myself, rather than you receive a letter from the health department."

"I'll watch for it, I don't want mom to find it. When it comes, I will go to the free clinic and be tested too."

"Don't wait for the letter Mary, go and get tested right away. If you're clean, you don't have to worry."

"I might have to worry anyhow Crissy; Nick also paid me extra to not wear a condom. You seem to have started feeling sick pretty fast too."

"The Doctor told me this AIDS virus is a rare one. If someone gets it, there are no symptoms for a while. When it does start affecting your system, it makes you feel like I have been feeling very fast."

121

Crissy looks at Mary's face, she tries to comfort her, and "I really dreaded having to tell you Mary. We are not the best of friends, or the worst. I didn't want getting sick to affect our friendship."

Mary wipes tears from her face, "I just can't stop feeling responsible that you got infected Crissy."

Crissy glances at her watch, "Please try to not feel that way Mary. Call me if you need to talk. I have to get back home and finish telling mom now."

"You told your mother what you just told me Crissy?"

"I was beginning to tell her Mary, I didn't finish telling her my story, now I have to go home and finish it."

Crissy gives her a hug she drives away. Crissy takes in a deep breath and drives back home.

Crissy walks in her home, Laura is in the kitchen, "I'm almost finished cooking dinner Crissy, sit down. Finish telling me what in this world is going on with you."

Crissy looks at Laura, "Let's wait until after dinner mom, then we can talk without interruptions."

Laura sit is a plate of food in front of her they eat in silence. They finish dinner and sit together on the couch.

"I started telling you mom; my weight loss is not the result of a crazy diet I was on. I am not intentionally starving myself or anything else.

Jan went with me to the free clinic; I wanted her with me because she is my best friend. I thought it was the right thing to do. The Doctor told me mom I have hepatitis C; it's treatable, with medications, and diet."

"Hepatitis C, the Doctor's positive about that?" Laura asks with a puzzled look on her face.

"The Doctor had his lab double check my tests to be sure. I have already picked up medicine I need at the free clinic pharmacy. This won't cost you or our insurance anything."

"Crissy, you should go see our family Doctor and get a second opinion. Do you know how you could have gotten Hepatitis?"

"Of course not mom," Crissy folds her arms across her chest, "I just want to be as well as I possibly can.

I have no idea about how I might have gotten hepatitis. The Doctor suggested I could have had contact with someone who had hepatitis, and somehow I got it from them."

Laura gets some water, "Will the Doctor notify anyone who had contact with you Crissy? You and Jan have been together a lot recently, and you just came back after being with Mary."

Crissy wipes tears from her face, "Only if they had direct contact with my body fluids from a sore, or injury but that hasn't happened. Since Jan and I have been close, she had a blood test too, which was negative. Your not in danger, nor is Jan, Mary or any of our family. The Doctor gave me pamphlets about hepatitis to read. When I'm finished, with them I'll give them to you."

Laura manages a smile, "When you said you had an emergency Crissy, I started imagining all sorts of things. You are acting, and talking like this is not a big thing Crissy. Hepatitis affects your liver, this isn't something to brush off Crissy, and it could threaten your life."

"The Doctor told me that mom, I didn't mean to make you think it isn't a big deal to me, it is, I'm sorry, I'm very scared, and upset."

"I still want you to see our Doctor, Crissy. He could verify the free clinic diagnosis, and then I'll leave it alone."

She sighs looking at Laura "I'll call and make an appointment mom. It has been a very long day. I'm really tired, so I'm going to bed."

She watches Laura turn on the television and sit on the couch.

Crissy calls Jan when she gets in her room, "Hello Crissy, did you tell your mom everything? If she finds out from some else, you will have to explain to her why you didn't tell her in the first place."

"No, Jan, I only told her that I had hepatitis C. I chickened out telling her I have AIDS.

The Doctor was more worried about Nick, Jim, and Mary, not mom Jan. Right now, I have too many things worrying me. I will tell her Jan, but not yet. I already told her the free clinic gave me medicine. I know she will worry, no matter what. The medicine should help me to start feel better, that will help her to relax enough for me to tell her about the AIDS."

"When are you going to talk to Mr. Junkett, Nick, Jim, or Karl?"

"I'm not really sure Jan; I don't have Nick, or Jim's number to leave them a message on voice mail. I do not have the courage yet to talk with Mr. Junkett in person. I don't want to talk to Karl; he probably would deny everything anyhow."

"So you're just going to let the health department contact all of them?"

"I don't know Jan, my head is hurting, and spinning, my body aching.

I need to rest a few days I'll decide then what to do."

"I won't lecture you about what's right, or wrong. You should have told your mom everything; If she finds out you risk losing her trust that you didn't tell her everything first."

"Your right Jan, I know that. You are my best friend and have been trying to tell me what I know is right. I face a death sentence. I just don't know how long it will be until it's carried out."

"Crissy fight for your life, you'll have to adjust to live the best and the fullest you can."

She starts crying "I won't ever be able to marry, or have kids Jan, I should just take a big hand full of sleeping pills and not wake up."

"Please, Crissy, don't say that, killing yourself wouldn't solve anything."

"Sorry Jan, I will go back to the free clinic. The Doctor can prescribe me something to help my depression."

"Do something positive for yourself Crissy, including talking with the Doctor about your suicidal thoughts. If he agrees you should take medication for depression, then he will give you something that will help you. Tell others your personal story about being and escort. Tell them about having unsafe sex and how doing that will affect the rest of your life. Doing that might stop even one person from becoming an escort. If someone listens to you Crissy, then you accomplished something positive."

"I will give that serious thought Jan. Right now, I don't know how to face the embarrassment of telling anyone about being an escort."

"I understand, and I'm glad I didn't get involved."

Crissy manages a laugh, "There will be an opening at Mr. Junkett's Jan."

"I wish I could laugh at that Crissy, but I can't, no thanks."

"Are you going to finish school Crissy?"

"Like you said Jan, I need to live my life to the fullest. Yes, I will finish, and I will graduate."

"Just don't go crazy and take pills. You're my friend, we will fight this together."

"Thanks Jan that means a lot to me. I need to rest now, good night and much love to you."

"Much love to you too Crissy, I'll talk to you later."

Chapter 15

A month passes; Crissy is gaining weight, and beginning to stabilize.

"Have you been back to the free clinic for a check up with the Doctor, Crissy?"

Crissy smiles at Jan, "Of course Jan, the Doctor and nurse are both pleased with my progress."

"I've noticed that you are looking better. You have some of your glow back Crissy. Have you made a decision about talking to other students about the risks of becoming an escort?"

"I still can't find the courage Jan. I want to, believe me I do. I'm still fighting depression and thoughts of wanting to take a lot of pills and not wake up."

"I thought we both agreed you weren't going to say anything more about committing suicide Crissy?"

"I have thoughts Jan, just thoughts, I didn't say I was going to commit suicide. I talked to the Doctor some more about my suicidal thoughts. He prescribed medicine to help my depression."

"You still have time, Crissy it won't be long until we graduate. If you talk to others now, it might prevent someone from thinking about becoming an escort."

"Right, just a little over two weeks left and we're finally finished with high school."

They walk together from their class, watching other students rushing to class, or ending their day. "What about Mr. Junkett, Nick, Jim, or Karl have you heard anything from them Crissy?"

"I went to Mr. Junkett and told him Jan. He said he would take care of it. I was there talking to him when he received the health department letter. He became so mad at me, he didn't open it."

"Has Jim tried to contact you Crissy?"

"No, I talked with Mr. Junkett the weekend before I was to meet with Jim. Mr. Junkett said he would tell him I was quitting and he would try to find another girl. To say the least Jan, he wasn't happy I had worked for an agency too. He cut our talk short, and told me to get out. I have not heard from him, since then. Jim or Nick's only way to contact me is through him. I won't answer my phone if Karl tries to call me."

"One good thing came out of your meeting with Mr. Junkett. You don't have to look for another girl for him."

"I wouldn't have considered looking for another girl even he had asked me Jan."

"Have you seen Mary? I've been looking for her, she seems to have disappeared."

"I left her a message on her cell about a month ago, she hasn't called me back. She has been really depressed, more than I've been Jan."

"I really hope she'll get help, or is getting help Crissy. I suppose she isn't working either?"

Crissy smiles, she pats Jan's hand, "I have my suspicions she's might still be working for that damn agency. That's her problem, I thought she would have learned after everything happened to me, maybe she hasn't?"

"I would have thought that to, I know being with you, hearing what the Doctor said, certainly scared me. It made me thankful I didn't go any further, despite needing more money."

She looks at Jan, tears fall from her eyes, "Jan, you were real close to working as an escort. You probably would have worked as an escort, if she hadn't returned. I still feel horrible I ever tried to get you involved."

"Please stop feeling that way Crissy. I did not get involved. Nothing we do changes our past; all we can do is work to change the future."

"It would be a good idea if we both go and talk with Mary. We can both try to encourage her to get help for her depression Jan."

"I'm alright with that Crissy, call her and see if she wants us to meet her somewhere. If she does let me know and I'll be there."

"Did you ever tell your mother the whole truth about what you're going through Crissy?"

"I've tried over and over Jan, and there again I lose my courage, I can't bear to see the disappointment on her face."

Crissy rubs her hand, "I have you, my dear friend, Jan, and you're here for me. You have not been judgmental, nor have you abandoned me. My greatest fear is someone finding out I have AIDS. I have to find the courage to talk with my father too, Jan. Thinking about telling mom everything has been rough enough. She needs to know from me how I got sick. I lied Jan, and I hate myself for lying to her.

I have always had an open dialogue with mom. She will be very hurt that I did not explain everything fully.

I need her on my side, and then she will back me up when I talk with my father."

"At least the stigma of AIDS isn't what it was Crissy, my mother told me gay people were the first to be diagnosed with, HIV, and AIDS. Now, anyone not practicing safe sex is at risk. The media has been telling how its spread and how you can get it."

Crissy glances at her watch, "I had better get going, and you should go home too Jan, I'll be in touch with you when I hear from Mary. We will go see her together. First, I will talk with my mother, and tell her everything, I promise."

"Alright Crissy, you have been with me when I needed you. If you need me to be with you, let me know."

"I appreciate that Jan; this is something I need to do by myself, for myself."

Jan rides home thinking, "I shouldn't lecture Crissy getting more courage and tell everything to her mom. I haven't even found enough of my own courage to tell my mother."

Jan goes into her home; Judy is talking on the phone. She hangs up, "Important phone call mom?"

Judy looks at her with a serious frown, "A friend of a friend just finished talking to me, and said they have been hearing a nasty rumor Jan. Have you, or your classmates heard any rumors at school?"

She puts her backpack down, "No one at school is saying anything, at least I personally haven't heard one. Did this person tell you what nasty rumors are going around mom? "

"It involves Mr. Junkett Jan, and girls who worked for him. Are you sure you don't know anything that you want to tell me?"

Jan gets a sick feeling she looks at her. "Did you think I know something about him or the girls?"

Judy moves closer to her, "I told you a long time ago there should be no secrets between us Jan."

Jan bows her head, she feels that Judy knows everything she has to tell her, "I don't know what to say mom, obviously someone is spreading a rumor, and it might be only a rumor. Why don't you tell me what it is, if I know any facts, I'll tell you, I promise."

Judy gets up and walks into the kitchen, she pours herself a glass of water, "Would you like a glass of water too Jan?"

Jan shifts her body nervously, "Yes, I'll take some water mom."

Judy sits down near Jan, she hands her a glass of water, and "I won't say who Jan, but someone calls me today and tells me a girl who worked for Mr. Junkett has very serious medical problems. Is that girl Crissy?"

Jan looks away from Judy, "Crissy is sick mom, and she has hepatitis C."

Judy keeps looking at Jan, "Anything else Jan, because I feel you know more than your telling me, your keeping secrets."

"I hate to keep secrets mom, especially from you. I had also promised Crissy to keep her secret. I have that dilemma of disappointing you, and her."

Judy rubs her hand, "I'll tell you what Jan, just tell me what you do know, and I promise that it goes no further."

"Did this person who told you the rumor say just how Crissy got sick mom?

Judy's face becomes a frown. "The rumor is that Mr. Junkett has been operating an escort service out of his business. It was told to me that he arranges for men to meet teenage girls for sex."

Jan feels her face become red and knows she cannot hide it; "It isn't a rumor mom; he is running an escort business. Crissy and another girl were involved."

Judy gives her hand a gentle squeeze, "Jan, were you involved too?"

Jan gives Judy a shocked look. "No, I wasn't, Crissy asked me to consider it when we first began school. A girl who quit went back to work for Mr. Junkett."

"Is that the reason you asked us for permission to work? So if you got the opportunity to do that type of work Jan, you would have?"

Jan bows her head, "Yes mom that was the reason. I could not because he would not consider me until I turned eighteen. Crissy also asked me to work with her for an escort agency that sent girls out to meet men. I just could not do it mom. By then, I had found the job at Mr. Clark's and I didn't feel comfortable, or right about selling my body to some strange man."

Judy goes into the kitchen for more water. She returns, sitting next to Jan "Who was the other girl Jan?"

She nervously rubs her glass of water, "Mary, remember, she gave me a hundred dollars for my birthday?

It was her way of bragging about how much money she was making at Mr. Junkett's."

"Any other girls besides Crissy, and Mary work for him or the escort agency Jan?"

"Not that I know of mom, Mary introduced Crissy to Mr. Junkett, who hired her after she left."

Judy sits back on the couch, "I want you to tell me more about her medical problems Jan."

Jan wipes tears from her face, "A total of three men paid her more so they didn't have to wear condoms Crissy met two men at Mr. Junkett's and one through the agency She could have gotten AIDS and hepatitis from any of them."

"Oh my, didn't she ask any them to show her they had been tested and were clean Jan?"

"She said that Mr. Junkett insisted his clients have current tests showing they were clean. Mary also had unsafe sex with the same man at his place for extra money. Crissy said the agency client she met, did show her his health test results when they first met."

Judy looks at her, "I want you to know Jan, that you could have told me about this long ago. I also understand that you did make a promise to her. You were being torn apart by right and wrong."

Jan smiles, "I've had a tough time trying to keep from telling any of this to you, I knew if you found out you would be very disappointed in me."

Judy smiles, "I would have been more disappointed in you, if you had became an escort Jan. You didn't, so I must say I'm very proud of you standing up for your morals.

Has Crissy said anything to her mother yet Jan?"

She looks away from Judy, "I asked her about that, and so far she only told her about having the Hepatitis, not AIDS."

Judy shakes her head in disbelief, "I suggest you try a little harder convincing her to tell her mother everything."

Jan nods her head in agreement, "I asked her if she's heard from Mary, neither of us has seen her at school. She got very upset when Crissy told her that she was infected. Crissy said Mary thought she was blaming her, but she wasn't."

"It was Mary who asked Crissy to work at Mr. Junkett's and the agency. It was her choice none of the men did not wear condoms. Mary shouldn't feel that she should be blamed for Crissy getting infected."

"Your right mom, it was Crissy's choice. Mary told both of us that she felt horrible. She felt that if she hadn't asked Crissy to be an escort, or work for the agency, then none of this would have happened."

Judy pats Jan's hand, "Still Jan, there were choices. She chose of her own free will to take that step. No one forced her, and no one encouraged her."

Jan wipes tears from her eyes, "Still mom, both of them are depressed, Mary more so than Crissy."

"Mary shouldn't feel that way; she didn't tell Crissy if she talked to anyone about her feelings?"

"I doubt it, she hasn't been at school lot, she has missed so many classes that she probably won't graduate with us."

"Is Mary sick too Jan?"

"No mom, very depressed, from what Crissy and I know. She stopped talking to both of us after Crissy told her she was sick, and what she has."

"Her mother could have found out, she could have gotten a phone call like I did, confronted Mary, and taken her to get help somewhere out of town."

"I have no idea mom, Crissy and I have both called her cellular, left messages, called her home, left messages, and she hasn't called either of us back yet."

Jan hears the honking of a car horn; she looks outside her window, "It's Crissy mom; I'm going to go talk with her thanks for listening, and your support."

Jan walks outside; she gets into her car. "I really need to go back and ask the Doctor at the free clinic to give me something stronger that will help me with my depression."

"Crissy, a pill, or pills only makes you feel good for a short time, when the effect leaves your right back where you started from."

"I'm still venting Jan; my world has come crashing down on me. I'm trying to dig out from its rubble."

"At least talk to both of your parents, and tell them everything Crissy."

"Telling everything to mom is bad enough to think about Jan, much less telling my dad."

Crissy squeezes Jan's hand, "At least you listen, then you offer suggestions Jan, I appreciate that. I wish both of us could talk to Mary. We need to find out where her head is."

"Maybe that is why she is missing classes and school; she could be getting help Crissy? If she is, I support her getting it. If she is still working full time for that damn agency, then I cannot support her. Do you know what has happened to Mr. Junkett? The clinic Doctor told you he might be contacted by law enforcement."

"He is out of business Jan. Rumors and the gossip going around the community put him out of business.

He has a business-closed sign on his building. No one in town has seen him since he got the health department letter. I think he is on the run, maybe from the law. I'm glad he didn't find any other girls to work for him."

"That is exactly why you need to talk to students Crissy, they might listen."

"Peer pressure huh, Jan?"

"Give deep thought Crissy, about talking to your mother, father, and the students. Could you at least do that not for me, but for yourself, and others?"

"I promise to give it my deepest thoughts Jan. I need to go home now; while I drive I'll think on it."

Jan leans over giving her a hug; she gets out of the car. "I have faith in you Crissy; I know you will do the right thing."

Crissy smiles at Jan as she drives off.

Chapter 16

Crissy drives back home slowly, getting courage to tell her mother everything. When she arrives home, her mother's car is in the driveway.

She walks in her house; Laura is sitting on the couch watching television. "There you are Crissy; I was getting worried about you."

"I had a long talk with Jan mom, and now I will tell you everything. I am not sure you are going to understand. I need to get a lot off my chest."

"Crissy, I can see by the way you're acting, you're stressed. I will listen to you, like I always have."

Crissy takes in a deep breath, "Mom, I didn't tell you the full truth about my illness. I took a friends place after she quit work and made a whole lot of money."

"I know that Crissy, wasn't it Mary who asked you?"

"Yes mom, it was Mary. She worked at Mr. Junkett's I watched what she did. I did not tell you he was running an escort service for his clients."

"Escort, you mean he talked Mary and you into being escorts, Crissy?"

"Both of us made our own decision about being escorts, he never talked us into it."

"How many men did you have to be with Crissy?

"I met two men there. "

Laura shifts her position on the couch looking at her.

"So, helping his clients was selling yourself to them Crissy?"

Crissy takes a Kleenex; she wipes tears from her face, "That is what I did. The man wanted to bring a friend. Mr. Junkett asked me to find another girl for him.

I asked Jan if she would meet with his friend; however, he would not consider her until she was eighteen. Mary returned before her birthday. Jan found work at Clark's Pharmacy, and never worked for him.

Mary told me an escort agency was hiring. We both worked with them too. I met a man through them, he double paid me to meet only him outside the agency, and triple pay if he didn't have to wear a condom."

"Did any other girls besides you and Mary work for Mr. Junkett, or the agency Crissy?"

"Just us, we were the only two."

"Crissy, you're beating around the bush. Did you get sick while working for Mr. Junkett?"

"I should have said illnesses mom when I first started talking to you, please just listen to me. The free clinic took tests for everything, and I have AIDS along with Hepatitis. I had unsafe sex with three men, I'm not sure which of them I got Hepatitis C, or AIDS from".

Laura sits for a few moments in stunned silence. She moves across the couch giving Crissy a hug. "You're my daughter, Crissy. I have offered you unconditional love, and support all your life. I still offer that to you and do not judge you. I wish you had made other decisions, just as much as you do. My support is to help you get through this."

"I really appreciate that mom, Jan offered to be here with me, but I needed to tell you alone. Another problem I have, is telling dad everything."

"Yes, I know Crissy; I know you don't want to tell him, but you have to."

"I didn't want to have to tell you everything mom, I worried that you would be so upset with me."

Laura hugs Crissy then says, "A mother has instinct Crissy about their child, and I felt that you were not telling me everything. I knew you would tell me, when you were ready. I cannot speak for your father, about what he might say or do."

"I can only ask you mom, will you go with me when I talk with dad?"

"Of course Crissy, I would not let you go by yourself. Besides, if your father knows my concern is you, and your health, do you want me to call and tell him we need to talk to him?"

"I will call him mom, and tell him that both of us will meet him. He already knows I've been sick."

Laura glances at her watch, "He is still at work, call him at his home, and leave a message. I hope he will call us back tonight and agree to meet us Crissy."

"I will mom, before I call him, I need to call Jan She will be happy we talked today. She has been very supportive of me and I owe her that."

"Yes, she has Crissy, what a dear friend she is at a time like this. Call her, and then call your father Crissy."

Crissy calls, "Jan, I've told mom, and she was wonderful and supportive. She will go with me and talk to dad, if he will meet us tonight."

"I'm so happy Crissy that is wonderful news. You need your mother to support you now, and in the future. Did your mom have an opinion about your dad's reaction Crissy?"

"No telling Jan, it can go either way. He could go ballistic, or will give me his full support."

"I will hope for your sake, and your mother's that he will support you Crissy. Please remember that if you need me, I'll be there for you too."

"You're my best friend Jan, I appreciate you so much and you know that. Don't be offended, this is something that I need mom to be with me and him."

"I'm not offended Crissy, I understand this has been horribly hard on you."

"I know Jan, now I need to call him and leave him a message. I will call you later on, no matter what and tell you what happens."

"Bye for now Jan, and much love to you."

Crissy hangs up her phone; she dials her father's number. She anticipates his voice mail but is surprised when he answers, "Crissy, how have you been doing? I've been so worried after finding out that you've been ill."

"I'm doing alright dad, mom and I need to talk with you tonight. Are you available for us to stop by?"

"What time were you thinking Crissy? I came home early to finish some office work here. I will make time for you. I just need to eat."

"Would seven be alright for us to come over dad?"

"That would be a good time Crissy, and tell your mother to not worry about me, alright?"

"She isn't that worried about you, she worries more about me."

"I worry about you too Crissy, despite your mother and our divorce, your our daughter, and sick. You're both of our concern, equally."

"Let's not have any disagreements dad; we will see you at seven."

She hangs up her phone, and returns to the living room.

"What did your father say when you told him both of us want to talk to him Crissy?

"Actually, almost pleasant mom, I was surprised. He will make time at seven, so let's eat mom."

Laura looks at her in disbelief of how he reacted. "His reaction must be because you're ill Crissy. If you weren't sick he would have come up with some lame excuse."

"I ask dad, and asking you mom, let's not have disagreements, or arguments. Now isn't the time for that." Laura gets up, going into the kitchen, "Your right Crissy, I will restrain my anger at your father. You show me a good example of that."

"I talked briefly with Jan, she wishes us luck mom."

"I knew she would Crissy."

"She offered to be with us, but I told her that this is something I needed to do just with you mom."

Laura smiles at Crissy while preparing their dinner.

They finish dinner, wash the dishes, and put them away. Crissy nervously glances at her watch. The ring of the phone startles Crissy; she gets up and sees her father is calling.

"Hello dad, can we still come over to talk to you?"

"I've finished dinner, so anytime is good Crissy."

"We will see you soon dad, and thank you again."

Laura walks out of her room, Crissy is hanging up the phone. "Did your father cancel Crissy?"

"No mom, he is ready, let's go and get this done."

She takes Crissy by the arm; they walk out of the house to the car. Neither of them talks as they drive.

Laura drives up outside his house, she looks at Crissy, "I just want you to know, that no matter what your father says Crissy, you have my full support."

She smiles at Laura, giving her hand a squeeze; they get out of the car. She waits for Laura, taking her arm they both walk to his front door.

Laura pushes the doorbell and waits, the door opens "Come on in," Crissy's father steps aside as they walk in. He gives Crissy a big hug and a kiss on her cheek.

Laura extends her hand to him "Thank you Paul, for doing this."

He smiles, but says nothing, and they both walk in to the living room and sit together on a large couch.

"Either of you want anything to drink?

"Bring us glasses of water Paul, and a box of Kleenex."

He returns sitting both glasses in front of Crissy and Laura.

"I have an extra box of Kleenex here," he reaches to a table by the couch.

He sits on a smaller couch across from them. "You look like your doing better Crissy. You have good color in your face, and look like you have gained back some of your weight."

She takes several Kleenex, "I'm trying dad, but there is a reason I needed to talk with you tonight. You're aware that I worked at Mr. Junkett's for a long time?"

"You seemed happy working there Crissy, and made better than average money."

"I've told mom, and now I need to tell you what kind of work I did for him. First, I must say it was my decision, and mine alone to work there. I also worked for another company, without telling him."

"Did he fire you for working for someone else Crissy or getting sick?"

Crissy wipes her eyes looking at her father, "Dad, I quit working for him. He hired Mary first; she worked as an escort at his place every weekend."

He sits up fast on the couch leaning towards her, "Escort, is that what I think it is Crissy?"

"I'm afraid so dad, Mary quit, I watched her. I started working as an escort after she left.

"So Mary quits, how many men did you work with at Mr. Junkett's Crissy?"

"Two, he wanted to bring a friend. Mr. Junkett wanted me to find another girl; I asked Jan if she would consider working. She could not work until she was eighteen. In the meantime, she returned and I started meeting with his friend. By then, Jan had found a job as a pharmacy technician trainee."

Crissy takes a drink of water. She looks at her father trying to judge his reaction. He is still listening to her, but has no expression on his face.

"Mary and I also worked with an escort agency where I met a man; he seemed nice. We had a strong attraction to one another. He paid me more to see just him, but not through the agency."

"Mr. Junkett had the men at his business show both of you health test results Crissy? What about the man from this agency?"

"He had one dad, it said he was clean. He offered me a lot of money to have sex without a condom. I wanted so badly to save enough money to pay for several years of college, that I accepted his offer."

"What about the men you were with at Mr. Junkett's Crissy, did they wear a condom?"

"They offered me more money if they didn't have to wear one.

I was with all of them until I began not feeling well. I went to the free clinic, they tested me and I tested positive for hepatitis C, and AIDS dad. The clinic Doctor thought since both men did not wear a condom; I could have gotten it from either of them."

He sits in silence for a few moments, "They could have scanned an older good report, and used a computer program to change it Crissy."

"I know dad, any of them may have faked their health report, and put a current date on it."

He sits silently looking at both of them, "Your mother and I have had our share of disagreements, and I haven't always been there for you Crissy. I take personal blame for not talking with you at the beginning of your junior year about how we would send you to college. Now that your fighting for your life Crissy, I'm not about to abandon you."

She begins to cry harder as Laura hugs her, He gets up and hugs both of them, they cry together. Laura looks at Paul, "There will be a lot of gossip, and rumors Paul. If Crissy has both of us standing with her, and behind her, she can live a productive life."

He sits back down, "Crissy, I hope you will get therapy. You're not crazy; you need professional guidance to help you cope with your illnesses."

"I will get therapy dad, which I promise to both of you. I really appreciate you not belittling me, and thinking bad about me dad."

Her cellular phone rings, "Crissy, this is Kathy, Mary's mother, is it possible that either you, Jan, or both of you could come over to our house right away?"

"Is something wrong there?" Crissy asks.

"I'm not sure, I've been knocking on her bedroom door for the past two hours, and she won't answer me."

"I'll call Jan then both of us will come as soon as we can Kathy."

Crissy looks at her parents and says, "Mary isn't answering her mom, she locked herself in her room. I need to call Jan and both of us go over there right now."

"Of course Crissy, call Jan, and tell her what she told you."

The ring of Jan's cell phone startles her and Judy, "I just talked to Kathy, Mary's mom Jan, she said she locked herself in her room and won't answer her. Her mom begged for us to come over there and see if we can get her out and talk her into going and getting help."

"I'll get there as fast as I can Crissy, it might take me an hour riding the bus, hold on I need to tell mom." Jan puts her phone on hold, "Mary's mother called Crissy, she insisted we need to come to their house to see if Mary will let us take her to get help. She isn't answering her mother, or opening her bedroom door."

"Of course Jan, did you want me to drive you over to Crissy's?"

"Yes please it will save us a lot of time mom."

Judy picks up her purse. "Tell Crissy I'm driving you to her house, I'll take both of you to Mary's house."

Jan takes her phone off hold, "Crissy, mom will drive me to your house, pick you up, all of us will go to Mary's."

"Jan, meet me at home as fast as you can. Her mother really sounded concerned, and I do not blame her."

Chapter 17

Judy and Jan rush out to their car driving as fast as they can to Crissy's house. She's waiting outside for them and waves when she sees them approaching. She quickly gets into the car,

Judy starts driving to her house.

"Thanks so much, Judy, Mary's mother was very upset."

Judy looks her rear view mirror at Crissy, "I have to wonder why her mother didn't say something before this?"

Crissy looks at Judy's reflection in her rear view mirror, "She could have thought Mary was under a lot of pressure being a senior and getting ready to graduate."

Judy drives up in front of her house. Kathy is looking through the window. They get out of the car, walking up to the door, "Thank all of you for coming so fast, I'm still not getting any answer from Mary."

Judy, Jan and Crissy walk with Kathy to her door.

Crissy tries to open it, it's still locked, "Mary, Mary, its Crissy, and Jan, we need to talk to you, please open your door, please let us in we're here to help you."

Crissy pounds her fist on her door, Jan tugs on her arm; "We should call 911 and have the fire department come."

Kathy looks at them, "If the fire department breaks down her door, and she isn't in her room she would be very upset."

"Kathy, I'll call 911, she can be angry at me. Has she been taking sleeping pills?" Judy says.

"She started taking them to help her sleep all night several months ago. I hope she did not take more than one they are powerful. Make the call Judy, I don't feel right about this."

Judy takes out her cell calling 911, the operator answers "911 what's your emergency?"

Judy looks at Kathy; Crissy is still pounding on her door. "We're not sure; a friend's mother called my daughter and asked us to help her daughter. She has locked herself in her room, and doesn't answer her door."

"I can send the fire department if you believe her daughter might be at risk in her room."

"Her mother has been trying to get her to respond for the past several hours. The past fifteen minutes all of us have been here trying to get her to open the door, getting no response. We do believe she might be at risk operator."

The operator pauses, "Is there any reason to suspect the girl is suicidal?"

I'll ask, "Kathy, has Mary said anything about suicide?"

Kathy wipes tears from her eyes, "No, she hasn't, she has been very withdrawn Judy. I have tried many times the past months to get her to tell me exactly why; she refused to talk to me."

Jan and Crissy are standing out side her room pleading for her to open the door.

"Her mother said her daughter hasn't threatened suicide, or hinted she was thinking about it. She has been very depressed and withdrawn is all we know. Please, the fire department needs to come here right now."

Judy gives the address and directions to the 911 operator.

Crissy still crying stops pounding on her door, Judy, Kathy, and Jan follow her to the living room.

The sound of approaching sirens startles everyone. Kathy runs to the door and waits.

A police officer comes in first, followed by a firefighter holding a large axe. "You're the mother who called for the fire department to help your daughter? Can you tell me what might be her problem?"

Kathy wipes tears from her eyes, "My friend called you, I've been trying to get my daughter out of her room for the past several hours. My daughter's friends came here at my request. They have not been getting a response from her since they arrived. I asked them to call for emergency help, since I'm not sure she is conscious."

The police officer writes down what she says.

The firefighter asks, "Where is her room?"

Kathy points to it, Crissy, and Jan stand up, "We'll show you sir, just follow us."

They walk fast to her room, pointing to her door.

The police officer pounds on her door, "Police officer, and open your door please. I need to make sure you're alright."

The police officer puts his ear on her door; he looks at Kathy, "What's her name?"

"Her name is Mary, officer."

The officer looks at Kathy "Please wait in your living room and let us take care of this."

Crissy takes Kathy by the arm and sits her next to Judy and Jan. Crissy stands in front of her.

The police officer again pounds on Mary's door, "Mary, open your door, we're here to help you." He waits, and hears no response. He motions with his hand for the fire fighter to hit the door with his axe. He swings his axe towards the knob; it falls off, the door splinters. The officer carefully pushes the door open.

Kathy jumps up and runs towards the door. She looks inside and does not see Mary on her bed. Puzzled she starts to follow the officer and firefighter into the room.

She sees a piece of paper on Mary's desk.

The officer puts out his arm and stops Kathy, "Please stand back; I had better see what's written on this note."

The firefighter takes Kathy by her arm, pulling her outside Mary's room.

The officer begins reading, "*My life is not worth living, I have hurt everyone who cares about me too much. I became greedy, lost control, and feel I have no future beyond this moment. I want to tell everyone that my decision on how to make money was a very wrong one. I am fully responsible for my friend getting sick. I want to say I am sorry, very sorry for everything, especially all of the disappointment I leave behind. I wish I could go back, and change so many decisions. This is a lesson to other women or girls that they risk everything becoming an escort. It was always about just about the money. I had my whole life ahead of me. I could not bear the thought of how others would look at me, think about me, or feel about me. I felt when everyone found out I was an escort, they would think of me as nothing less than a whore, and slut, who sold her body for money. I could not bear the burden any more. I cannot find any reason to continue and to live.*

Mom, I am so sorry to leave you, and dad, I love you both. I always will. Mary."

The officer hands the note to the firefighter, he hands it to Kathy. The officer looks under her bed He looks in her bathroom, and inside her closet.

Crissy and Judy hold on to Kathy, crying with her. She finishes reading the note; she crushes it into a ball throwing it towards a trashcan.

The officer opens her door, motioning for the firefighter to come inside. The firefighter pardons himself and goes into the room. After a few moments, he comes out with the officer they approach Kathy.

The officer and firefighter both remove their hats, "We're very sorry to tell you it appears to us that Mary wrote the note, placed it on her desk. She went into her closet, put a belt around her clothes rod. She placed the belt around her neck and let herself go limp."

Kathy looks at the officer and says with disbelief. In her voice, "She's dead; my precious daughter Mary has killed herself officer?"

The officer bows his head, "We have to call the coroner they make the final determination on the cause of her death. Please go into the living room and sit on the couch." Jan, Crissy and Judy take Kathy by the arm and lead her to the couch. They all cry together. Judy watches as more firefighters come into the house looking into Mary's room, walking out with a sad look on their faces.

Crissy finally says, "Kathy, we're all so very sorry, I should have tried to contact Mary earlier. I thought she was going to get help."

Kathy glares at Crissy, "Were you working with her?"

Crissy looks away, she looks back at Kathy, "Yes, we worked together, we were both escorts Kathy."

More police officers come into the home.

An officer approaches Kathy, "I'm Lieutenant Brent, my job is to try to help you through this, the best I can. The coroner will be here soon to investigate. They will be taking Mary to their office for a more through examination. I do grief counseling. I'm here if you need to talk."

Kathy looks up at him, "She's dead, what more talking can you do?"

Judy takes Kathy's arm, "Let's go outside Kathy. We do not need to be in here when the coroner arrives. You shouldn't watch them take her out." Jan, Crissy, and Judy walk her outside; some of her neighbors are standing around watching and wondering what has happened.

She looks at them, "Go home, please, if you must know, my precious daughter Mary killed herself today." Judy takes her by the arm and they walk a short distance from the house, "Kathy, I hate to bring this up, but what do you want for Mary, a funeral, cremation, a service?"

Kathy wipes tears from her eyes, "Mary had always asked that she be cremated, and her ashes scattered at sea. She could not bear the thought of burial.

I'll find a funeral director to arrange everything after the coroner is finished."

Crissy walks over to her, "If you have a memorial service for Mary may I speak at it and tell those who attend that their choices in life will affect themselves if they make the wrong choice."

Kathy takes a few steps from Jan, Crissy, and Judy, and looks at them, "That's a good idea Crissy, just do us one favor, don't bring up the escort thing. I would prefer that part of her life to remain very private and confidential."

Crissy looks at her, "I respect that Kathy, but try to understand if other girls out there are considering it, they risk everything, I know that fact well, and I'm infected with diseases I never wanted. My greed overpowered my common sense too."

Jan looks at her, "If I may add my opinion, word will leak out that she killed herself, and was an escort. If Crissy is brave enough to tell their story without mentioning her name, it could save a girl, or woman from getting into that business."

Kathy approaches Crissy, gives her a hug, and says, "Say what you feel is necessary Crissy."

Crissy, Jan, Judy and Kathy watch as the coroner arrives and do their investigation, then they take a gurney out of their truck and take it into the house.

Kathy says, "This is good bye Mary, I'll try to make your life worth something, despite you feeling it wasn't."

Jan, Judy, and Crissy give Kathy a hug together. The coroner removes her body and leaves.

Lieutenant Brent walks up to Kathy, "We're finished here, the coroner will advise any funeral director when her body is ready to be released; here is my card, so please call me if you need me."

Kathy looks at his card, "Thank you so much, but I have my dear friends here to help me with all of this, and together we will get through it." Jan, Judy and Crissy stay with Kathy, while she phones relatives and informs them of Mary's death. After Kathy finishes calling everyone she could, she sits on the couch with a dazed look on her face.

Kathy looks at Jan, Judy, and Crissy, "I should have seen this coming; Mary withdrew so much the past months, not talking to me, not talking to her friends, then just dropping out of school."

"Kathy, I have had my own issues with depression, and if you asked Jan, she would tell you more than once I mentioned killing myself. I'm still depressed, but I've began to know by opening up, talking to girls, women who might want to consider being an escort, then I can use my particular situation to save a life. I feel that would honor Mary more than anything."

Kathy looks at Crissy, "I admire your courage, and you understanding the repercussions of doing that Crissy. I am feeling so numb right now, but somehow I feel her spirit in this house and she is telling me that if we keep her alive in that spirit, and give one another courage, then we all can put out a message. As you said Crissy, it might save another life.

I began to suspect something when I saw her with so much cash. I questioned her about that, and she avoided answering. When you got sick Crissy that is when she finally told me, she had worked as an escort. I was more than shocked, and wanted to pack up, move and not tell a soul where we went. It was even more shocking when I found a letter she had opened and probably dropped it, or forgotten it. It was from the health department advising her to get a health check up."

Kathy wipes tears from her eyes, "I didn't want anyone to know, but this small town, it was inevitable someone would find out. I begged her to stop working, and she told me she had. I feel she finally convinced herself that everyone knew she was an escort, and that she had asked you to work with her Crissy."

Crissy gives her a hug, "I'm not sure a lot knew, but someone sent out anonymous letters."

"Mary started to tail spin more and more, I feel now that she made up her mind that she had no other alternative other than killing herself. I appreciate your strength and courage Crissy in wanting to talk to other students, and their parents."

"I'm at the point where I could care less what they think of me Kathy; it is saving their child that gives me my strength and courage."

"It's wonderful that you have great friends who stand with you Crissy."

Crissy looks at Jan, and Judy saying "If it had not been for them Kathy, I would have killed myself. I was that desperate many times. I will honor her memory, she was our friend, we loved her, and she loved many people. That should matter, more than the work she did, or how she died."

Jan and Judy smile at her and say, "We want to establish a foundation in memory of her, the money raised will pay to educate others, and the risks they face by being an escort."

"I'll mention that in my speech tomorrow, we all need rest, let's go home." They all give Kathy a hug telling her to call if she needs them.

Chapter 18

Because of her courage, Crissy is her class valedictorian and speaking at June graduation. She walks up to the podium, looking out at her class. She sees Jan, Judy, Kathy, and Laura smiling at her in the front row.

Pausing a moment, *"Our senior class graduates in the loving memory of our classmate Mary. She would have wanted all students, parents, teachers, to make her life mean something. She lived a short life and all of us here today; can save others, in her memory."*
She wipes tears from her face *"My name is Crissy, I became an escort. I contracted AIDS and hepatitis C by having unsafe sex. I now face living the rest of my life on drugs to control my AIDS and hepatitis, I do not know if I will have a short life, or a long one. I decided my mission in life is telling the message about Mary, honoring her, and her short life. The power and greed for money has me standing here before you today. Mary's mothers, my mother, and many wonderful friends are establishing a foundation in her memory. If being brave enough talking to everyone here today is not enough, look in your own mirror. I hope you can find you own way to be brave, non-judgmental. I see myself as one of you, your daughter, your cousin, your niece, your sister, and your friend. I have found many reasons to live. It's your choice class, parents, friends to make your choices be the right choice."*

She accepts her diploma, wiping tears from her face. Everyone who listened to her speech joins her in tears and applause.

Kathy walks up to her, "What you said Crissy was so beautiful. Thank you for honoring Mary, and being here for others."

Laura gives a hug to Kathy, "We all share your pain and loss Kathy. Crissy said it best; Mary was a friend, a daughter, and one of us."

Crissy wipes tears from her eyes. Everyone in the crowd is crying.

The class finishes graduation; each student gives her encouragement to continue her quest of getting the truth out. When all of her classmates finish, teachers offer their hugs, encouragements, and congratulations for speaking out.

"Your father is here Jan." Judy says.

She sees him standing the distance. "I will go talk to him and thank him for coming, and not intruding."

She gives Judy, Crissy and Kathy a hug, and walks over to her father.

Judy watches, "He knows this is a special day for her, he won't make a scene."

Kathy gives her hand a squeeze, "We know that, Judy, let her handle him."

Judy smiles at Kathy.

Jan spends fifteen minutes with him, she walks back, a smile on her face, "Dad understands we all need each other, He offered his deepest sympathy to you Kathy."

Crissy gazes out over the crowd, she sees her father, "There is my dad too Jan, I'm going to go talk to him." She walks over to his hug, "Crissy I'm so proud to be your father, I'll do everything I can to help you." Crissy holds on to his hug with tears falling from her face.

She kisses her father and walks back to join Kathy, Jan, and Judy.

The principal walks up to her, "Come and see me in a few weeks Crissy, I have sources that are offering you grants that will pay your college education in full."

He looks at Jan, "That applies to you too Jan, I'm aware that you want to become a pharmacist I would love to see you accomplish your career objective."

Judy looks at them, "You two were so worried about acceptance, or rejection, and now you're finding out about understanding. The reward for your courage is getting grants."

Kathy holds on to Laura watching Crissy and Jan pose for their graduation photos, smiling and laughing. They feel emptiness inside themselves without Mary standing beside them.

THE END

www.ingramcontent.com/pod-product-compliance
Lightning Source LLC
Chambersburg PA
CBHW051830170626
46807CB00003B/1104